THE WATCHER IN THE DARK

He followed Anna at a discreet distance. Because of the darkness and the fog, he nearly lost her a couple of times, finally drew closer than he'd intended and watched her go into a door marked 117.

Skirting the bright patches cast by the wall-mounted security lights, he made his way to the corner of the building until he stood near the door she'd entered. He edged past it to the long front window and positioned himself to look through the narrow slit left by the incomplete closing of the drapes.

The room was lit. He could see his quarry seated near the back wall, and seconds later another person crossed his vision, brushing the draperies so that they parted, letting the light fall across his startled face. He darted to the side, back into the shadows.

Not tonight, then. The boss said to take her quietly, attract no attention.

He would have to wait … but not for long.

LISBETH CHANCE

BAJA RUN

TOR

A TOM DOHERTY ASSOCIATES BOOK
NEW YORK

BAJA RUN

Published by arrangement with Walker Publishing
Company, Inc.

A TOR Book
Published by Tom Doherty Associates, Inc.
49 West 24 Street
New York, NY 10010

ISBN: 0-812-50132-2   Can. ISBN: 0-812-50133-0

Library of Congress Catalog Card Number: 86-5482

First Tor edition: December 1988

= 1 =

HE'D BEEN WAITING barely an hour, and already boredom was beginning to take its toll. He yawned, then stretched, wishing he had a thermos of hot coffee to take the edge off his fatigue. Forty hours was a long stretch without sleep, and he had at least another ten or twelve to look forward to.

A heavy fog, what the natives called *bruma*, had rolled in only minutes earlier, a thick, soupy mess that had saturated everything within seconds and left him feeling chilled. Condensation rolled down the outside of the Huey's windshield like rain. It definitely wasn't a typical night in balmy Mexico.

He shifted in the pilot's seat, straightened his left leg and winced. His knee was stiffening up again, and the scar throbbed with an old, familiar ache. Maybe walking would loosen it up; at any rate, it was as good a way as any to kill a little time. Climbing from the cockpit of the helicopter, he stood in the sand for a moment, glancing around the island to get his bearings. He couldn't see more than a few feet, but he knew the main house was to his left, the jetty directly ahead a few hundred yards, and the small cove behind him. He headed for the cove.

The sound of the surf was muted, though it wasn't more than ten feet from him; the sea fog was a blanket, cutting the small island off from the rest of the world like a wall. It wouldn't make any difference now, he thought, if he did get clearance to leave. Until the fog lifted he was landlocked. *Wait for the wind*, he told himself hopefully. The *bruma* was only an occasional occurrence, but the few he'd seen were always short-lived, blown away by the inevitable wind that followed the fog.

For perhaps fifteen minutes he walked, the feel of the sand underfoot somehow reassuring. It wouldn't be hard to let imagination get the better of you, he mused; this was the perfect setting for nightmares or fantasies, depending on your frame of mind. If given a choice, Donovan would opt for the fantasies. He had enough nightmares to deal with in the daylight.

Forcibly steering his mind away from what could be a troublesome course, Donovan stopped walking and schooled himself to absorb the tranquility that surrounded him. It was a well-practiced discipline, one he'd used often in the past fifteen years. But tonight it wasn't working. There was something there, just at the edge of his awareness, not threatening, more like an intrusion. As though he were being watched . . .

It was when the wind began to rise, rustling the oleanders and parting the mist, that he saw her.

She was standing at the edge of the breakers looking at him, so still he might almost have missed her. Whipped by the wind, her long, white skirt molded her slender body like a man's caress, and for one incredulous moment Donovan wondered if he were looking at a sea nymph. She raised her arm; he thought she was beckoning him, but instead she pushed away the hair tangling around her face.

He was never sure who took the first step, but it was unimportant in the long run. They were simply there, face to face, so close he could touch the tears running down her cheeks, brush his thumb across her mouth, and he did. Even beneath the heavy mane of hair, her skin was cool against his fingers, yet when she placed her palms against his chest, the heat seemed to sear through his damp shirt. When he held her in his arms, her heartbeats jarred his body; when he kissed her lips, he tasted the salt of her grief and felt the urge to cry with her and lessen her burden.

6

When he lowered her to the sand, a brief flash of recognition first startled, then soothed him, like a well-loved ritual—he *knew* this woman and this act. Then the *bruma* closed around them and Donovan stopped thinking.

"Hey, Donovan, wake up."

Groggy and wet, Donovan sat up in the sand and shook his head to clear it. He looked around. The fog was gone and so was the woman.

"Funny place to sleep," Crewe continued, giving the peculiar wheeze of laughter that never failed to set Donovan's teeth on edge.

"You're telling me," Donovan muttered. What the hell had happened?

"What's the matter, Ace? We been workin' you too hard?" He wheezed again. It occurred to Donovan, not for the first time, that Crewe was easily amused.

"Stuff it."

"The ace is touchy. Anyway, you can go now. We've decided to stay through 'til Monday." The man's short, stocky frame looked a bit misplaced in the expensive gray suit, but he withdrew the fat wallet from an inside pocket with familiar ease. "This oughta cover the charter, plus down time."

Still somewhat fuzzy headed, Donovan was slower than usual to reach for the crisp bills Crewe extended.

"I can be back late Sunday."

"Better wait 'til you hear from me," Crewe said.

"Something big going on?"

Crewe managed to convey both sly delight and disappointment. "I'm surprised at you, Ace. You're not usually so nosey."

Donovan was a little surprised himself. He knew the rules and followed them: don't ask questions, just fly. But then, this whole night had been a surprise. "Whatever. You know how to reach me."

"Yeah. Don't take any—"

"—wooden *pesos*. I know."

Chuckling at his stale joke, Crewe disappeared back into the oleander bushes toward the main house, leaving Donovan to count his pay and try to clear the cobwebs from his head. A reddish lightening of the sky told him it was nearly dawn; he'd been on the island at least five hours, only about two of which had been given over to sleep. Maybe the long days and longer nights were getting to him—could it have been a dream?

He discarded the notion. No dream had left that taste in his mouth—the flavor of a woman's lips. And no dream had put that faint smell of perfume into his clothes. Another look up and down the beach confirmed what he already knew—there was no slender blonde woman with wet, sandy clothes standing spectrelike in the dawn.

Irritably he began the walk back to the helicopter, trying to concentrate on the business at hand. He had a charter in Guaymas at noon, which left him just enough time for a meal and a bath, so the sooner he got into the air, the better. Pausing one last time to look around, Donovan shrugged. What was it his landlady had told him once? "Strange things happen in the fog. I myself have seen the spirits of sailors walking the beaches during the Festival of the Dead. Most unsettling."

Unsettling indeed, but he'd held no ghost in his arms last night. Most likely she worked on the estate, or perhaps she was visiting. He'd heard old man Michelotti had died—could be she was here for the funeral.

He remembered again how she'd felt in his arms, wondered if Crewe would know anything about her, decided that asking would be too risky. Crewe's last-minute jobs paid a good portion of the bills, but the cardinal rule was "no questions." "Pretend you're a deaf-mute," Crewe had told him once; "all we want is your eyes and the chopper." There were times, like now, when he hated the life he'd chosen, hated the characters like Crewe he was forced to deal with. He knew what Crewe and his associates were—

criminals—and he knew too that no matter how careful he was, there always existed the chance that he could be tainted by their activities. But like somebody once said, life's a bitch and then you die. He'd put up with it because, right now, he had no choice.

He climbed into the cockpit and started the engine. While whipping the sand into a frenzied cloud, the thumping rotors calmed him. To the east, the dawn sky brightened, and he inhaled with pleasure. Soon he would be in his element once more.

Anna could feel herself unravelling as she tugged frantically at the skirt, finally ripping the fabric before it dropped in a sodden pile around her feet. She didn't know how much longer she'd be able to hold herself together.

It was just too much to deal with—first, Poppy's death, then that incomprehensible episode on the beach after the funeral, and now this . . .

A brief struggle with the buttons on the flimsy camisole top seemed endless, calculated to make her crazy.

'Tavio. It was incredible that he would be part of anything like this. Eighteen deaths, all directly attributable to the man she'd planned to marry. She remembered when the story broke, only a few weeks ago; every newspaper and television commentator had screamed the gory details, flashed the pitiful photographs of the dead Mexicans in an obscene contest of sensationalism. The only omission had been the identity of the runners responsible for taking those eighteen people into the desert to avoid the *federales*, then abandoning them.

Now she knew who was responsible. How could he? He had been her friend, a part of the family, nearly all her life. But she couldn't deny what she'd just overheard. What would she do? What *could* she do?

Eighteen people dead . . .

Several more precious moments ticked by while she rummaged through the chest of drawers for a clean shirt and jeans. She resolutely avoided the huge mirror above the dresser, knowing what she would see: a thinness so pronounced that the hollow of her collarbone was a deep shadow on her skin; dark-blonde hair matted and gritty proof, if she needed it, that the disgraceful encounter on the beach hadn't been a hallucination; she would see a narrow face strained beyond recognition—the reflection of a stranger.

Where was the real Anna Michelotti? This frightened, confused child bore no resemblance to the woman she thought she was, the woman she wanted to be. As she fumbled with the suddenly obstinate zipper on her jeans, she allowed herself the brief luxury of a few more tears, then she lifted her chin stubbornly. "If crying will change things," her grandfather had once told her, "then cry. If not, then do what must be done to survive."

Noble words, great advice, but how the devil was she to do it? Poppy hadn't told her that, and now it was too late. He was dead. Everyone was dead, it seemed, even 'Tavio, who was alive and boldly strutting around with his plotting and backstabbing and devious plans, up to and including her own elimination, if necessary. *If the girl should become a problem, she will be dealt with.* She shivered. If he were to find out that she knew . . .

Her shirt was on, though not precisely in place, and she grabbed a pair of tennis shoes from the closet and crammed her feet into them. A lace broke when she yanked at it, and she sobbed, her demoralization nearly complete. "Poppy," she whispered into the still-dark room. "Come back, just for a minute. Tell me what to do."

Instead of her grandfather's voice, she heard 'Tavio's.

"Juana, have you seen Miss Anna?" Did his melodic tenor, which she had once found so appealing, now carry an ominous note, perhaps a threat?

"I saw her go into the study, *señor*, perhaps ten minutes ago."

Anna stood motionless until the footsteps receded, one

pair toward the servants' quarters, the other toward the south wing. A sudden and involuntary realization chilled her: she was afraid of 'Tavio, afraid of the man she had agreed to marry. Above the stillness of the great house, she could almost hear the fluttering of her heart, like a butterfly trapped in a jar.

She counted to a hundred. Then—carefully, quietly— she crept to the French doors that opened onto the terrace. Behind her, she heard the bedroom door open.

"Anna? Anna, wake up, I need to talk to you."

For just a moment she wavered, wanting desperately to trust his familiar voice. But she couldn't, mustn't, face him now. One look at her face and he would know. Her only chance to stop him, maybe her own safety, lay in getting away.

Darting across the flagstone, she slipped into the trees. 'Tavio's voice rose above the rustle of the foliage and pursued her. "Anna, where are you?"

The path she chose was now overgrown, but she still knew its every turn and pitfall as well as when she'd played there each day. A vine snaked around her foot and she shook it loose, stumbling to lose a precious second. The oleander bush she'd hid under on her seventh birthday— God, had it really been twenty years?—loomed to her right, an ominous hulk in the semidarkness. Something sharp scraped against her arm as she flew over the ground, but she shrugged past it, not slackening her pace.

Her feet moved with a sure swiftness, racing to the urgent message that pounded in her brain:

Run, Anna, run . . .

She was in the launch when the realization hit her. The key! She'd forgotten the key. And her handbag. *Fool!* she cursed silently. What else had she forgotten?

She looked around the cove helplessly. The waters were tranquil, only the tiniest motion disturbing the smoothness, ocean and land blending together in a gray monochrome. An almost palpable silence covered the island, but she knew it was a deceptive quiet. The house would be in turmoil by now, the sounds of running feet and urgent calls filling every corner of every room. She couldn't go back, only forward.

As she hopped over the side of the boat into ankle-deep water, her palm slipped. Sweat, she thought, then noticed the dark smear of blood her fingers had left on the chrome railing. For the first time she noticed the small gash across her forearm. Of course, the palmetto. She only vaguely remembered falling into it; even now she was aware of no pain and pushed it from her mind. She would tend it later, when she was safe.

But when would she be safe? Where could she go?

Think, Anna!

The jetty, that was it—there would be an outboard at the jetty. She began to run.

It was lighter now. In a few more minutes, the sun would be up. Maybe she should duck back into the bushes, lessen her chances of being spotted. 'Tavio would have given the alarm by now, and every man on the estate would be looking for her. But no, she couldn't make time dodging trees and climbing through vines, so she would stick to the shoreline.

A sharp stab of pain tore through her ankle as it twisted and she sprawled headlong into the sand, biting her tongue hard when she landed. The taste of blood gagged her and she nearly retched, then recovered.

Hurry, Anna, hurry . . .

Pushing to her feet, she tried to run again, faltered, settled for a limping trot. It wasn't much farther now—she was coming out of the cover onto the long stretch of beach on the south side of the island. Encouraged as much by fear as by the nearness of her goal, she limped faster.

She saw the copter first, then realized she'd been hearing it for several seconds. Already the rotors were whirling; soon it would be airborne. She had no idea who might be in the cockpit—perhaps one of 'Tavio's men—but she would have to risk it. Running in earnest now, she shouted, "Wait! Don't go. Damn it, wait for me!"

Donovan twisted the throttle and smiled slightly at the sound of the engine changing pitch. He knew every knock, whirr, thump, thud, and clunk the machine could make. She was running fine today. In fact, everything was shaping up fine. His run in Guaymas would take six hours tops, then he could get some sleep. It wasn't often he looked forward to unlocking his ratty, minuscule apartment, but right now he could hardly wait to feel the mattress underneath him, lumps and all.

He looked to the side and saw her in the same instant she pounded on the door. Torn, dirty, and blood-streaked, her hair whipping wildly into her mouth and eyes, she looked more like a Poe nightmare than a human. Nonetheless, he recognized her, and something inside his chest gave a peculiar little lurch.

He breathed an oath, a pungent Arabic word he'd picked up in his misspent youth, not knowing if the epithet was a comment on his reaction to her appearance or to her being.

The man in the house was disturbed, his dark features marred by a frown as he listened to the excited chatter of the servants who scurried from room to room.

How much had she heard? he wondered. No matter. Anything was too much. The more important question was, what would she do with the knowledge? A hint, the merest whisper, would be enough to wreck the entire operation, and if the operation went, so did he. *El Patrón* had made it clear.

He rose from the leather chair with a jerk, paced to the window and back, his high brow furrowed under the black, shiny widow's peak.

"Of course I can handle the girl," he'd boasted into the phone. "Don Roberto had the eyes of an eagle, and we kept it from him. Why should his granddaughter suspect? She is a soft nothing, completely inexperienced. She will be relieved to have someone of my caliber to administer the estate."

El Patrón would remind him of those words when he was told of this incident.

Again he paced. How foolish he'd been to discuss it in this house that was filled with so many ears. He would have to watch himself more carefully—it was clear he had a tendency to let his self-confidence override caution, and that kind of mistake could be deadly.

It was regrettable that Don Roberto had left the Family for more legitimate enterprises. In the old days the Don would have run the operation himself and these needless deaths would never have occurred. But he could not deal with what might have been. The girl was an immediate concern, one which demanded decisive action.

Taking a *cigarillo* from the small agate box on the desk, he tapped it nervously several times before lighting it. Perhaps he was overreacting. It was possible the little fool was simply running from her grief; during the funeral she had been near the breaking point.

He abandoned the thought. That would have been out of character for *la princessa*. The old man had taught her well. She would always meet her responsibilities with squared shoulders and a regal smile, as befitted a Michelotti. Only shock or fear would cause her to run away, and his telephone conversation would have amply provided her with both.

Methodically he went over every word of his call to *El Patrón*, every statement, overt or implied, every nuance of tone.

La verdad, he concluded. She now knew it all, and that knowledge would, unfortunately, endanger everyone concerned. How ironic it was: when he had told *El Patrón* that the girl would be dealt with if she became a problem, he'd been referring only to financial matters. She had obviously put a much different interpretation on the remark.

He shook his head. *Que lástima.* By her own actions she would bring her fears to terrible life. If only there were some other way. He abhorred the taking of life, but there were times when it was unavoidable. It had, for example, been necessary to order the execution of the cretins who had botched the last shipment and left all those illegals to die in the desert; one must maintain order and discipline. Now it was just as necessary to ensure the silence of one Anna Michelotti . . .

She was probably hiding in one of her ridiculous childhood "castles." There were at least a dozen such places scattered over the island. If so, Crewe or one of the others would find her. If not, she couldn't get very far.

Either way, he would know soon.

= 2 =

ANNA DARTED A sideways glare at the man in the pilot's seat, feeling like a battlefield for a silent war between fear and anger.

The full impact of her situation hadn't registered until they were airborne, and now she felt wretchedly vulnerable and stupid. All the signs had been there, but she'd been reacting, not thinking; now she was as good as imprisoned with a man who must never, under any circumstances, know who she was or why she so desperately wanted to leave *Sonrisa*. It would be tantamount to walking straight into 'Tavio's arms.

She had recognized him immediately, of course, and a joyous relief had buoyed her up. He would help her, she would be safe now. But disillusionment had set in at once, followed closely by a numbing disbelief. After his initial surprise at seeing her, a closed expression had settled over his features. He had looked at her as though he'd never seen her before, and a chilling suspicion took root in her mind.

He was on the island for a specific reason, but in the throes of panic she'd failed to recognize the implications. Now she faced them head on. Either 'Tavio or one of his "business associates" paid this man for services rendered. He could even *be* one of those associates.

She'd rallied quickly, deciding to play his game of nonrecognition. If she could retain her anonymity and talk him into taking her off the island, she could be back in the States in a matter of hours. She began by trying to be reasonable . . .

* * *

"I just need to get to Santa Marta," she pleaded. "It's only a fifteen-minute flight." The flap of the rotors made normal conversation impossible, and she felt a fool shouting over the din.

"Fifteen minutes one way," he countered, "and that adds up to half an hour, plus an extra fifteen or twenty in and out of the airport. Sorry, lady, but my charter in Guaymas is too important to risk missing."

More important than my life? she wanted to scream. "Okay," she bargained recklessly, "I'll pay you. How much?"

"The charter's a sure three hundred. Then there's the inconvenience. Say five hundred."

He obviously expected the price to discourage her, but at that point Anna would have agreed to almost anything; she expected to feel 'Tavio's hand on her shoulder any second. Darting around the Huey, she wrenched open the door and pulled herself into the empty seat.

"Wait a minute. That's five hundred up front."

His words stunned her. "Do I *look* like I've got five hundred dollars on me?"

"To tell the truth, lady, you don't look like much of anything, and I don't have time to debate the issue. So if you don't mind . . ."

She wanted to slap him, wipe the disdain off his hard, set face, but she retained enough control to know she couldn't afford to lose her temper, not now.

"Please! I'll go to the bank as soon as we land; you can go with me. It'll only take a few minutes. If we hurry, you might even get back to Guaymas in time for your regular charter."

"Banks aren't open this early."

Anna gritted her teeth against this obvious logic. "All right, I'll call my friend Josefa. She'll loan me the money."

His strange, amber eyes flicked over her coolly, and she hoped, just for a moment, that he was beginning to relent, to see her as a fellow human being in need of help.

"What kind of trouble are you in?"

The second he asked, the first alarm went off in her head and she knew she mustn't tell him. "I'm not in trouble, not like that. I mean, there's been a death in my family and I've got to get home." The awful truth in the lie hit her hard and, against her will, she began to cry softly. "I just need to get home."

"Couldn't someone up at the house arrange something for you?"

She shook her head, trying not to panic yet again. "I don't like to impose on my—employers—and besides, they've got troubles of their own." Certain that he would know of the death on Sonrisa, she felt not mentioning it would be too obvious an omission.

Whether it was her argument or her tears that swayed him, she didn't know, but he merely shrugged, though even that neutral gesture somehow conveyed his scorn. "Whatever. But you don't move farther than two feet away from me until that money's in my hands."

She stared at him in disbelief. She hadn't expected a lifelong commitment from him, but after the warmth, the tenderness they'd shared on the beach, his coldness baffled and chilled her. Why was this happening?

Now they were approaching Santa Marta, and every passing mile had only reinforced her disgust, not only with him but with herself as well. She was too fair-minded not to admit her own culpability in that eerie interlude on the sand, but under the circumstances it became easier, even desirable, to direct her bitterness toward him.

She stole another sideways glance at him. In profile, his could be the face on one of Poppy's old Greek coins, noble and refined, crowned with tightly curling brown hair, but what did that mean? Nothing. There was no nobility about him. He was a boor, insensitive to the finer emotions and apparently indifferent to her resentment.

The thumping of the rotors reflected her turmoil, drumming against her ears until she wanted to scream with frustration. *What now? What now?*, they mocked, and she clenched her fists against the urge to cover her ears and shut out the sound.

Once again she looked at him, longer this time, but neither by gesture nor expression did he betray any sign of interest in his passenger. *How*, she wondered dismally, *how could I have given myself to him? And how can he act as though it never happened?*

So great was her need for comfort that for the barest fraction of a moment she sought excuses for him: *Maybe he doesn't recognize you. After all, it was dark and you left him sleeping, without a word.* Then she recovered. It was a weak argument at best. Somehow she knew he recognized her. The awareness between them was almost tangible, in spite of their noncommunication. He simply chose not to acknowledge what had happened.

The admission was painful, but it had to be faced. Here was no hero, no shiny knight on a fiery steed coming to her rescue. Here was a potentially dangerous man who might be her enemy. The sad reality engulfed her. There was no one to take care of Anna now; she'd have to do it alone.

A traitorous thought sprang to mind—she could almost feel again the warmth of his body covering hers when she had been cold, so cold. He had warmed her . . .

Blindly she stared at the ultramarine waters slipping away below them. Someday, when she felt up to solving the puzzle, she'd ask herself why his rejection hurt so deeply, but now was not the time. She was too confused and, though she hated to admit it, too weak.

Her head suddenly throbbed with tension, and she rubbed grimy fingers against her temples as though to erase the memories. There were other, more important, problems. 'Tavio could be right behind them, even waiting at the airport when they landed. Or he could run her to ground before she got out of Santa Marta.

Which brought up another problem: how would she

leave town? Her cash, credit cards, everything, was in her bag back on Sonrisa. And in spite of what she'd promised that—*pilot*, she didn't dare go to the bank. It was one of the first places 'Tavio would check.

How had it all fallen apart so quickly, her beautiful world? Merely adjusting to the hole her grandfather's death had left in her life was a monumental task. He'd been her mainstay, her only family, and she was still learning just how much she'd depended on his strength. Now her anchor was gone, leaving her adrift in confusion and fear. She was six hundred miles from her L.A. apartment, her friends, the familiar security of the campus. 'Tavio, whom she had trusted, had suddenly become a monster. Her very life might be in peril. And she still had this man to deal with.

They were in sight of the coast now, but Anna felt she was looking at an alien world. The Sea of Cortez was the same, clear and serene, washing the barren beaches and cooling the summer sun; the land hadn't changed. It was still Baja, a rugged monotone of spines, ridges, and rocks, yet beautiful when you looked in the right places. But today it was dreadfully different. It wasn't home anymore.

She sighed, praying for the answer Poppy had always told her would come.

Donovan made the trip to Santa Marta in silence, too edgy to even attempt to deal with the woman sitting next to him. She was acting like a witch, and he, uncharacteristically, was letting it bother him. Maybe it was age or maybe just fatigue, but he'd been a jerk to let her rope him into this. Tears and money. They were a potent combination, but he'd resisted stronger stuff. He cursed himself in three languages for not having resisted this time, especially when his gut was trying to tell him she was running a scam.

But the memory of how she'd felt in his arms kept intruding on his common sense. Though he tried hard not to think about the episode, it haunted him, and he couldn't help wondering why she was so hostile. He certainly hadn't taken her by force, and by anyone's standards it had been a powerful experience.

Maybe too powerful? The question demanded attention. How much of that bull about "tears and money" should he allow himself to believe? Hadn't he himself done exactly what he'd expected her to demand of him, become involved out of a misplaced obligation, because they'd made love?

He'd been deliberately reserved when she'd first made her startling appearance at the helicopter, anticipating an emotional appeal that had never come. Now, instead of being understandably relieved, he was, perversely, irritated. He'd do better to stop thinking about it. Obviously, her feelings on the subject were radically different from his, but if she chose to ignore it, then so would he.

But it wasn't that easy to drop. Why were they both being so careful not to mention what had happened between them? He started to tell himself she was probably an old hand at tumbling strangers on the beach, then he remembered her tears, her unfeigned grief, and was unaccountably proud that it had been he who eased her pain.

He hadn't felt her glaring at him for several minutes and turned his head toward her. She was looking to the northeast at *Volcan Las Tres Virgenes*, some twenty miles distant, her face drawn with sadness. But there was something more. Fear? Desperation?

Stay out of it, Donovan, he warned himself angrily. *Your life is enough of a mess as it is. Don't add to it.*

But he knew he would find that advice difficult to take. If his hunch was right—and his hunches usually were—he had a whole potful of trouble sitting beside him.

As though she felt his eyes, she looked at him. Without the veneer, her face was soft and ridiculously innocent. He wanted to pat her shoulder and tell her not to cry. But then, suddenly, her mask was back in place, her lips thinned with dislike, and she seemed to dare him to offer her anything, especially sympathy.

The airport swept into sight below them, and Donovan turned his attention to the task of landing the Huey. While the whine of the rotors died away, he opened his door. "Time to deplane, duchess," he told her as he slid to the ground.

He watched the girl closely as she climbed from the cockpit and joined him on the tarmac. God, she was a sight! Looking at her in the full light of day, it was close to impossible to reconcile this ragged alley cat with the sensual woman of the fog.

Not that she had the looks you'd expect to find on a magazine cover. She was just a little too thin, her shoulders a little too broad, her not-quite-green eyes just a bit too widely spaced. In fact, if you looked closely, her face was subtly off-center. But her hair, thick and gold and soft, had felt magnificent in his hands; her skin was an unblemished ivory, and her mouth, wide and full, was made for kissing. And even now, eclipsed by dirty, torn jeans and a shapeless T-shirt, her body moved with a provocative, unconscious grace. He remembered how she'd felt . . .

When she stood beside him, he took her arm in what was intended to be the classic "light but firm" grip. She was no more surprised than he when his fingers tightened reflexively.

"Don't grab," she snapped.

"Just keeping in touch." Though he relaxed his hold, he didn't relinquish it. "You can call your friend from inside."

"Okay. But can I stop at the ladies' room first? I'd like to clean up."

He shrugged. "Make it quick."

Propelling her slightly ahead of him, Donovan caught the faint fragrance of her perfume and cursed silently. He'd remember this package for a long time, he admitted; everything about her seemed to turn him inside out, and he resented the intrusion.

The airport was small and all but deserted. Tourism was still new to this part of Mexico, so most of the generous

Anglos and Europeans still spent their money on the mainland. A couple of private planes were being fueled up, but the charter-company office, housed in a small trailer set apart from the main terminal, hadn't yet opened, so Donovan steered her toward the long, low building directly ahead.

Foot traffic in the terminal was sparse at this time of day, a fact Donovan noted gratefully. He wasn't anxious to be seen escorting a young woman who looked as though she'd been kidnapped and assaulted. He just wanted to collect his fee and get the hell out of Santa Marta.

"Go ahead," he told her when they reached the door marked with a small stick figure wearing a skirt. "And for God's sake, do something about your hair."

She opened her mouth, but thought better of whatever she'd started to say. Instead, jerking her arm from his fingers, she flounced through the door, then opened it again.

"I need a comb."

"Use your fingers."

"I said I need a comb! Don't you have one?"

He snapped his fingers. "Darn! And I really meant to bring it along."

"Why don't you stop being a jackass and do something constructive," she hissed. "Go see if you can find a vendor or something. And don't worry, I'll pay you back."

He nodded complacently, wondering if she really thought he was simpleminded or if she was just desperate enough to take the chance. He waited until the door closed behind her again, then moved down the hall a few yards and stepped around the corner to wait. He gave her fifteen seconds.

It was almost too much time. When he caught up with her, she was nearly out the east door of the terminal.

"You forgot your comb," he said softly into the back of her head.

24

Her knees buckled with reaction and she nearly fell, but when he tried to steady her, she whirled, her hands brought up to strike.

"Hold it, wildcat," he ordered, grabbing both her wrists. "Forget your way to the phone, too?"

"Stop it," she whispered. "Just please, *please*, let me go!" Now she was trembling, pale, no longer a jaguar but a frightened kitten. "I'm good for the money—I'll send it to you, I'll sign a note, anything. Just please let me get out of here!"

"I'd be more inclined to listen if you told me the truth. What the hell's going on?"

She shook her head stubbornly. "I told you, I have to get home. My family will be worried, they're expecting me . . ."

Disgusted, he jerked her closer. "I'm not a fool, lady, and I don't like to play games. In fact, I can't think of much I do like about you."

"Yeah, I guess I looked a lot better at two o'clock this morning," she flung back at him, "but then so did you!"

Her stricken face told him how bitterly she regretted the acknowledgement of their lovemaking; the stubborn set of her mouth told him she'd neither retract it nor discuss it; the tears swimming in her eyes told him she was close to breaking.

The depth of emotion that swept over him then plunged ruthlessly to his core, a fierce, deadly anger that anyone or anything would dare to hurt her this way. The anger faded beneath a bleak helplessness. He couldn't protect her because she wouldn't let him. She didn't want him.

If he had any sense at all, he told himself, he'd just walk away and leave her to whatever she was running from. But he knew he wouldn't. *You're a fool, Donovan. Get out while you can.* That was what he told himself, but he knew he wasn't listening.

"Come on," he said gruffly. "You're going to get cleaned

up, and then we'll find a phone. When I've got my money, you've got your freedom."

Anna hung up the phone, wondering if the fake conversation had convinced him. If he knew she'd been talking to a recording for the past sixty seconds, he might prove to be more than she could deal with.

Her companion looked at her, his eyes unreadable except for his obvious fatigue. "I take it the trusty Josefa is out."

Anna wished she could tell what he was thinking. Behind that carefully noncommittal expression, she feared, was a very dangerous man. And he was clearly exhausted, which would make him edgier and more irritable. Just how important would five hundred dollars be to him, and how far would he go to protect his interests?

"She went to the market. She should be back by ten." Did he believe her?

"By ten." He hadn't released her arm since the abortive escape attempt, and now he increased the pressure of his fingers, tangible evidence of his displeasure. "My patience is wearing thin, lady. I've about decided to take you back where I found you and push you out, preferably from a couple of hundred feet up."

She didn't doubt him. "If you've got a solution, I'd be glad to hear it. Otherwise I don't know what else to do but wait." His patience wasn't the only thing getting thin—her bravado wasn't faring too well, either. She was just plain scared, and each extra second spent in the terminal brought her that much closer to total panic.

"Anna."

The sound of her name, spoken in his gravelly voice, was startling. "What?"

"Just wondered if that was really your name. What's the rest of it?"

She wondered wildly how he'd found out who she was, nearly bolting through the airport with fear, before she

26

realized. Of course, he'd heard her on the phone, leaving a phoney message for her "friend."

"Well?"

"Well what?" She couldn't remember what he'd asked her.

"Your name, duchess."

"Mitchell. Anna Mitchell." Had she stumbled over the lie, hesitated too long?

"Anna Mitchell." He smiled, faintly but unmistakably, and shook his head. "Honey, you better learn to lie, or else go into a different line of work."

"And just what line of work do you think I'm in, *honey?*" She tried again to jerk out of his grasp, irritated with herself for being so easily nettled.

He tightened his grip, forcing her to bend her elbow, bringing her hand even with her eyes. "These hands don't belong to a housemaid from Sonrisa. Hell, your polish isn't even chipped. So whatever your line is, it calls for lying, and you're not very good at it."

"Let me go!"

Abruptly he dropped her arm. "Whatever. But until I get my money, we're going to be closer than Siamese twins. We'll wait until ten, but on my terms, so get used to it."

"Fine." Not for anything would she let him upset her again. Whatever his terms, she would deal with them. In fact, if they included getting out of this miserable airport, where she felt so exposed and vulnerable, she would stun him with cooperation. Looking as she did, she was bound to attract attention, and that was the last thing she needed. By now, 'Tavio surely had a small army of men scouring Santa Marta for any sign of her.

His next words were a spooky reflection of her thoughts. "Let's get out of here. I don't know about you, but I could use something to eat." In a betraying gesture, he rubbed his hand across bloodshot eyes as though trying to wipe away his tiredness.

She felt the first stirring of hope; if he were tired enough, he would, sooner or later, make a mistake. She hoped it would be sooner. "Okay." She shrugged carelessly. "There's a pretty good restaurant not far from here."

"Nope." His amber eyes, still expressionless, watched her. "I think a hotel room would be more comfortable, and a lot more private. Nobody to object if I have to tie you down to make you stay put."

Was he laughing at her? "You're wasting your breath, you know. I'm not afraid of you."

"Right."

He *was* laughing at her! *Just wait*, she thought, mentally gritting her teeth. *You'll screw up, fly boy, then we'll see who's laughing.*

There were a few taxis outside the terminal and all were empty. He herded Anna before him and pushed her into the first vehicle in line.

The sleepy Mexican behind the wheel listened to the gringo's terse directions while letting his gaze rest on Anna. She felt like squirming under his scrutiny, knowing that her haphazard attempts to straighten her hair had been less than successful. Then he aimed the dilapidated Chevy down the boulevard and stomped the accelerator, leaving the air filled with thick, white smoke.

"There's no hotel there," Anna accused.

He looked at her indifferently. "So what?"

"So you said we were going to a hotel."

"We are."

"But that's an intersection, and a shoddy one at that. There's no hotel."

"Maybe you just don't know where to look."

"Maybe you just don't know how to give directions."

"Maybe."

Since he obviously wasn't going to explain himself, Anna drew as far away from him as the backseat would permit and glared. "I think I have a right to know where you're taking me."

He turned his head deliberately and gazed out the window, seemingly absorbed in the colorful shop fronts speeding by. Anna almost admired him—that sort of cool reticence would have done her a world of good back on the island. She could have faced 'Tavio down, and he never would have suspected that she knew about him. As it was, every thought, every emotion, was clearly reflected on her face. It was something Poppy had warned her about, but until now she'd never really understood what he'd meant.

She found herself wishing she could read the truth in *his* face and know what kind of man he was. In spite of the fact that they'd made love—or something—she didn't know the first thing about him, not even his name.

"You speak Spanish very well," she probed. "You must have lived here for a while."

He ignored her.

"Do you live in Guaymas?"

He scratched his head.

"Do you come out to the island often?"

He yawned.

"Where did you learn to fly?"

"Pushy people annoy me," he said conversationally, startling her. "When I've been up for two days, like now, they provoke me. And when they divide their time between lying to me and trying to pump me for information, I become violent."

"Well, there goes the image of a man of few words," Anna retorted, then wisely kept her mouth shut for the rest of the ride. She needed to think anyway. He said he'd been up for two days, which confirmed her impression that he was almost literally dead tired. She'd also discovered that he could be goaded into anger if the right buttons were pushed. As she'd told herself earlier, a tired man would make mistakes. So would an angry man. Did it necessarily follow that a tired, angry man would make twice as many mistakes? Probably not, but it might be worth considering. How had Poppy put it? "There are infinitely more chances available to us than are ever taken, *carissima*, simply because we stupidly wait for the chances to take us."

Engrossed in fantastic plans for daring escapes, the immaturity of which she candidly admitted to herself, Anna barely noticed when the cab stopped until the driver turned to face them.

"*Aquí, señor?*

"*Sí. Que debo?*"

"*Quatro ciento y ochenta.*"

With one hand, her companion fished in his pocket for the pesos; the other snaked out to capture her elbow when she began sliding toward the door.

Reflexively she slapped his arm with her free hand, then held her breath when she realized what she'd done. But his retaliation never materialized. He just looked at her with those strangely colored eyes, and she knew he was laughing at her again.

As they exited the taxi the driver spoke, too softly for her to hear, then both men laughed. Anna recognized the sound—she'd heard it often in this country—as Latin *machismo* humor, one jerk congratulating another jerk on how well he handled his woman.

"Having fun?" she asked sweetly as he escorted her down the sidewalk.

"It beats hemorrhoids."

Neither spoke again but walked in a most uncompanionable silence. Anna began to view her surroundings with even more unease than before. There were no office buildings here, no bankers and secretaries hurrying to their desks. In fact, they'd passed almost no one, unless you wanted to count the two women who hung over the windowsill of a decrepit apartment house to toss a few good-natured obscenities at the drunk on the pavement beneath them.

Four blocks, two side streets, and one alley farther on, in the heart of what had to be the local *barrio*, Anna found herself entering a bleak, shabby building, which, in her opinion, should have been razed shortly after completion.

"This is it?" she asked incredulously. "This is your idea of a hotel? I don't believe it!"

He paid no more attention to her protests than he had before.

As they crossed the dark lobby to the desk, it occurred to her that she hadn't thought of 'Tavio and her own precarious safety in at least ten minutes. *If nothing else*, she thought almost fondly, *the man sure knows how to keep your mind off your troubles*.

== 3 ==

SHE'D GIVE THE room this much—it was the last, the *very* last, place 'Tavio would expect to find her. On the other hand, anyone looking for Donovan would probably make a beeline for the Victory Bar *Restaurante y Hotel*. It was definitely his kind of place, right down to the questionable stains on the putrid, green bedspread.

Who knows, she thought wryly, *it could be his regular suite*. Both the clerk and the hard-eyed beauty behind the bar had known his name, and judging from her reception, the barmaid probably knew quite a bit more than the clerk. It hadn't been hard to figure out: those dark sloe eyes had offered a lot more than the coffee Donovan had requested.

She watched him sit on the bed, his back propped up against the dirty wall, and open a greasy brown bag in which a half dozen *empañadas* resided. As always, his craggy face was devoid of expression, and she grudgingly applauded his self-discipline. The morning had been an ordeal for them both, and a frown or scowl, even a tooth-baring snarl, wouldn't have been inappropriate.

But since that one lapse in the terminal when he'd threatened to dump her into the sea, he'd wasted no emotion and very few words on her.

She wondered if he were a mercenary who'd traded the Central American jungles for less hazardous venues. She'd met a man on Sonrisa one summer, a business associate of her grandfather's, who'd had that same closed-in look. Poppy had later told her the man had spent nearly twenty years on foreign soil, fighting everybody's wars but his own.

At least she knew his name now, courtesy of the hotel employees. It was easy to think of him as Donovan. Not as expressive as several terms she could think of, but it suited him nonetheless. It was economical but definite, like the man himself.

This being the first time she'd had both opportunity and intent, she looked him over carefully (as much out of boredom as curiosity, she insisted silently) and found herself admiring his spareness. He was lean almost to the point of thinness, with a tightly coiled strength in his movements, a wary tension reflected in something as small as the tilt of his head. His face seemed to be all planes and angles, emphasized by a network of tiny lines at the corners of his eyes. Even in repose his mouth and jaw were hard, unyielding. If it wasn't a handsome face, neither was it unattractive. The total effect was of an animal tension, tightly controlled but purposely kept near the surface in case it should be needed.

When he stood abruptly and faced her, she realized he wasn't much taller than five-ten, though if she'd been asked, she'd have guessed six-one. His age, too, was difficult to determine; between thirty and forty was as close as she could come.

He raised one eyebrow questioningly, and she cursed the red stain that flushed her sheeks.

"I thought you were taller," she explained.

"I thought you were hungry," he responded.

"So did I until I got a whiff of that stuff. Are you actually going to eat those things?"

He nodded. "First and only course, so you'd better take advantage of it."

"No thanks. I've come to have a certain respect for my body. I wouldn't want to do anything to tick it off. There were some *pan dulces* at the next vendor's stall; why didn't you get some of those?"

"Why didn't you tell me you wanted some?"

"Why didn't you ask me what I wanted?"

"Why don't you climb on the bed like a good little girl and be quiet."

His tone hadn't changed, his expression hadn't altered, but she went all quivery and nervous inside. "What for?" she demanded, obstinately refusing to back down.

His mouth twitched in that half-smile she was coming to recognize. "I want you on the bed because it will be hard for you to break and run from a prone position," he told her with exaggerated patience. "And I want you quiet because I want you quiet."

Her palm itched to slap him. "I hate you."

"I know. It's part of my charm. Now get on the bed."

"Why can't I just sit on the floor? I promise I won't move an inch without . . ." Her radar detected the limits of his civility, and she complied, comforting herself with the promise that she'd think of something. One always thought of something when one had no choice.

Since the bed was shoved into the juncture of the walls, she pointedly climbed onto the mattress from the end rather than going across him, and she leaned into the corner, crossing her ankles and her arms.

Just as pointedly, he ignored her petulance and offered her an *empañada*. "They're no good when they get cold."

Her nose wrinkled itself in disgust. "You got the first part right. They're no good."

"You know," he said slowly, as though he were somehow surprised by this facet of her character, "you don't *look* like a picky person."

"*You* have no frame of reference for picky people. *You* patronize the Victory Bar, which effectively eliminates any possibility of meeting picky people."

Unexpectedly, he laughed. "You're a funny lady, Anna. I almost like you."

"Yeah," she answered, trying not to grin, "and I almost like *empañadas*."

35

For an instant a sort of harmony flowed between them, a rapport that teased with its nearness, then faded, eliciting uncomfortable memories of a shared intimacy. She felt oddly embarrassed, as though he could read her thoughts. "But not enough to eat one," she added and felt more foolish than ever.

Mercifully he seemed not to notice the awkwardness. "Then have some coffee. There's plenty."

"Uh-uh. I don't trust Carmencita's coffee pot. That stuff's probably brewed from equal parts of bilge water and love potion number fourteen."

He didn't pretend to misunderstand the remark, which surprised her. "Yeah, I guess she does come on a little strong, but then, the Americans who come in here seem to expect it. She's not a bad kid, just trying to earn a living. And her name's Kata."

Anna snorted. "She's not a kid at all. And she should be ashamed of the way she earns her living. We have too many misconceptions to fight down here as it is. Every tourist who comes into this place probably goes home to tell their neighbors about the really great time they had with your Kata."

The humor faded from his eyes, replaced by something she felt was scorn and outright dislike. "You sound like a spoiled brat. Kata has three kids to feed and nobody to help her do it. At least *she's* smart enough to stick around and collect her fee."

"What's that supposed to mean?"

He fixed her with that flat gaze. "You figure it out."

She already had, and the knowledge dealt her a numbing blow. His words cut too deeply to analyze, made her feel cheap and ugly. "That was uncalled for, Donovan." She paused to swallow the quaver in her voice. "You don't know anything about me, and I wish you'd just shut up."

Wearily he tipped his head back to rest it against the pillows piled behind him. "You're absolutely right, Miss Anna. I don't know a damn thing, and I think I'll just shut up."

Still stinging from his accusation, Anna nevertheless found herself battling the urge to apologize. Twice in less than a day he had helped her through a crisis—first in those icy, frightening hours after Poppy's funeral, then again when he took her from Sonrisa and hid her in this ratty room. So what if he hadn't exactly volunteered? A debt was a debt, and she'd given him nothing in return except hard knocks. There were times, she thought ruefully, when an innate sense of morality could be a purple pain.

Apparently Donovan was one of those maddening people who meant exactly what they said. The minutes ticked by, punctuated by the sounds of their breathing, the soft slurps when he sucked coffee from the flimsy paper cup, and the rising street noises of a wakening town. But he didn't utter a word. Not one.

Ten minutes later, she chanced a look at the man beside her. Head tipped back, eyes closed, the paper cup still held loosely in his long, straight fingers, Donovan no longer looked threatening. He just looked tired. His chest rose and fell rhythmically, though she knew he wasn't asleep. Yet.

The seed of hope that had been planted at the airport turned into a small bud. It would be such an easy, perfect solution. Once asleep, after so long awake, he'd probably be out for hours, then she could leave. No muss, no fuss, just walk out of the door. Then she could go back to Los Angeles and away from 'Tavio, give herself time to think and plan.

Here in Mexico, everything was on 'Tavio's side. She had no concrete proof of his guilt, and he had all the aces: power, a solid reputation, control of the money. If she accused him now, he could make her look like a hysterical fool; he could buy all the witnesses he needed. No, she could do nothing until the will was probated and she gained control of the estate. Then she would have the resources, the power. All she needed was time, and maybe she could buy a little of that with a phone call. That was it—she'd call him when she got back to Los Angeles, tell him she was overwrought with grief and just had to get away. She would plead for time to get herself together before they discussed wedding plans. He might not believe her, but it was worth a try.

Donovan moved, stretching his legs, but he didn't open his eyes. She waited silently. A few minutes later, he set the paper cup on the table beside the bed and slid farther down on the pillows, making himself more comfortable. Still she sensed his alertness, so she set out to alleviate some of the tension. Wiggling into a prone position, she yawned and turned on her side, cradling her head on her forearms.

She concentrated on taking deep, regular breaths while going over her plans one more time. Getting out of this room was step one; later she'd worry about step two—getting out of Santa Marta. It would be difficult, dangerous, but the stakes were worth it. She was, quite literally, fighting for her life, and for the lives of hundreds of unknown Mexicans who might entrust themselves to 'Tavio and his organization.

When she closed her eyes, she saw again the picture in the paper: bodies of men and women, even two small children, bloated and grotesque after several days in the desert. They'd been looking for a better life and had been served betrayal and death.

A chill settled in her stomach, a cold, hard knot of fear and despair. She wanted desperately to tell someone. No, not *someone*. Donovan.

She wanted to believe he wasn't one of the bad guys, but it was too great a risk. He'd been on the island, which meant he had some connection with either her grandfather or 'Tavio, but which one? If she guessed wrong, it could be the last mistake she'd ever make.

Drowsily she scooted her bottom closer to the comfortable warmth, sighing with pleasure and absently caressing the hand that cupped her breast. She didn't want to wake up, not yet, not while she felt this contented and safe and protected. As long as she could lie here like this, she'd never have to be afraid again.

Some more rational part of her brain signaled a warning: it wasn't a part of her routine to wake with a man's hand in possession of part of her anatomy. The rest of her gray matter, though, seemed lazy, indolent, not wanting to take alarm.

Several seconds later her eyelids flew open and she nearly groaned aloud. Behind her, Donovan snored lightly, his breath feathering the hair around her ear, his lean body pressed spoon-style against hers from knees to neck. He stirred, moved his hand from breast to waist to thigh, then squeezed gently while her lassitude made a quantum leap into frenzy.

Moronic, careless! Insanely irresponsible! She should have been gone by now. If he woke and caught her, she deserved it for being so utterly stupid.

But he didn't wake. While she lay motionless, afraid to breathe, he snored on. She exhaled with relief.

The next few minutes were an agonizing eternity. Only when she felt certain it was safe did she move, and then only in brief, careful stages—her head, then her shoulders, inching away from him in pieces. He stirred when she moved her leg, murmured a few unintelligible words, snored again. By the time she freed herself of his disturbing touch, she was damp with sweat and limp with exhaustion.

Then began the long slide to the end of the bed until, at last, her feet rested on the floor.

So far, so good. Now for the tough part. She wished for a radio, a fan, anything to provide some cover noise in the small room. But there was only the soft burr from Donovan and the muted hum of an occasional car from the street. To her ears, the silent fall of her sneakered feet on the frayed rug sounded like thunder, and she held her breath as she tiptoed around the end of the bed toward the door.

When she was level with Donovan's head, she paused. He hadn't moved. On his side, his back toward her, he slept on. She felt a brief regret that she had to leave him with no explanation or apology; he really wasn't a bad sort beneath that air of tough indifference. At any other time, in any other place, they might have been friends. Very close friends. More than anything else she could imagine at that moment, she wanted to trust him.

She shook away the thought and reached for the doorknob. Then she saw the wallet.

It protruded more than halfway out of the back pocket of his jeans, obviously pushed up from all the scooting and settling he'd done. Thin, trim, one of the trifold styles, it tempted her.

Never, not once in all her twenty-seven years, had Anna ever stolen anything. Quite simply, she'd never needed to. All her needs and wants had been provided, usually anticipated. Now everything had changed. She told herself the circumstances warranted becoming a thief. She told herself that Donovan would do the same thing in her place.

But it was a long, long time before she could bring herself to approach the bed.

Her fingers trembled when she stretched them toward the prize, and she snatched her hand back.

She tried again. This time she touched it; with thumb and forefinger she gave the smallest, gentlest of tugs. It was loose.

The next tug was the tiniest bit more aggressive; the wallet slid out another quarter of an inch.

Biting her lip and squeezing her eyelids tightly shut, Anna prepared herself for the final play. She inhaled deeply, counted to five. Then, as deftly as any surgeon excising a lump, she removed the wallet from his pocket and stood staring at it. She'd done it. She had actually picked a man's pocket.

Donovan gave no warning. In one fluid motion, he rolled, grabbed her wrist and was roughly jerking her toward the bed before her reflexes geared up. She braced herself, threw all her weight into a heave backwards, stumbled. As she hit the floor, dropping the wallet, Donovan was on her, shifting his grip from her wrist to her shoulder, cursing in a soft monotone.

With no conscious plan, she planted both her feet solidly in his belly, leaving him gasping for air. She gaped in amazement—she hadn't expected this. Scrambling upright, she lunged for the door, but not quickly enough—his fingers hooked her T-shirt, and she yelped with fear and frustration. Desperate and terrified, she whirled to attack. Her left elbow jabbed into his face, followed instantly by a swift, fierce, right-handed chop to his neck.

He sagged to his knees. As his head dropped, Anna caught his look of uncomprehended pain and found herself hurting with him. Her self-defense class hadn't prepared her for the damage she'd been taught to inflict. Blood streamed from his nose, red and garish; his eyes began to glaze.

"I'm sorry, Donovan," she whispered with a sob.

Then she grabbed the wallet, hating the feel of it, and left him there on his hands and knees in the dingy room.

As she ran along the dim hallway, she hoped she was going in the right direction. It was hard to see through the tears.

Octavio Herrera listened impatiently to Crewe's rambling explanation, clearly wondering why such a moron had been kept on the payroll for so many years. The man was an imbecile.

". . . she's just not here, *señor*."

"I gathered that," Herrera acknowledged. "If she is not *here*, Crewe, she must be somewhere else. In order to be somewhere else, she had to have left the island. It is a small island, Crewe, with limited means of transportation. Have you checked the boats?"

"One of the first things I thought of, *señor*. She didn't leave by boat. One of the men did find something, though . . ." Crewe faltered, obviously wishing it were anyone but he to deliver this news.

"*Cabrón!*" Herrera spat. "Say what you must and stop mewling!"

Crewe swallowed nervously. "The launch, *señor* . . . there was a smear of blood, fresh blood . . ."

Herrera's fist slammed against the desk top, leaving his knuckles starkly white. He lapsed into a stream of rapid Spanish that left the unfortunate Crewe pale and sweating. When Herrera's rage was spent, he questioned Crewe again. "That was all you found, just a smear of blood? There was no sign of a struggle?"

Crewe shook his head emphatically, his pasty jowls slowly returning to a more normal color. "That's it, *señor*. The tide's come in, so if there were any footprints in the sand, they've been washed out." He cleared his throat uneasily. "Uh, can I go now?"

"*Momentito*. This man who flew you out here last night— is he still here?"

"Donovan? Nope. I sent him back to Guaymas a good while ago."

"How long is 'a good while'?"

"Right about daylight."

Herrera's dark, highly arched eyebrows drew together in a frown. "Who is this Donovan?"

"Just a guy we use sometimes," Crewe assured him. "He's on the up and up."

Herrera glanced toward the third man in the room, who had been sitting unobtrusively in an ornately carved chair, saying nothing. "Santos, do you know this Donovan?"

"A local pilot, the partner of Felix Ortiz, I believe," Santos shrugged, rising to walk to the center of the room. He was a dapper man, small and distinguished with touches of gray in his hair and moustache. His voice was soothing. "Ortiz came to Guaymas after Vietnam, Donovan a year or so later. I believe they served together. Their business is legitimate, though not very profitable, and we've found them to be reliable and discreet." He clapped the younger man's shoulder with a firm, reassuring hand. "Be calm, Octavio. We will make inquiries of Mr. Donovan, but you will find your Anna has come to no harm."

"There is the blood."

"Which could have come from any one of twenty others on this island. No doubt she is merely reacting to Don Roberto's death. Perhaps she needed some time alone, chanced upon Mr. Donovan as he was leaving and persuaded him to take her on as a passenger."

"There have been kidnap threats several times in the past, when she was a child. I cannot help but worry."

"I know how distressed you are, Octavio, especially with the other problems that face you now. As I worked for Don Roberto, I will now work for you. You have only to tell me what you require."

Herrera regarded Santos coolly for a moment, then nodded. "*Sí*. I am grateful for your loyalty." He paused for a moment, as though considering his next move. "It would seem advisable to speak to this Donovan before we search further. Crewe, you know where he lives?"

Crewe nodded. "I'll take the launch to Guaymas. I can find out what he knows and get back to you in a couple of hours."

"Exactly." Herrera waved his hand in a gesture of dismissal, not bothering to watch Crewe as he left the room. "Santos, if you'll excuse me, I have some private matters to attend to."

"Of course," Santos acceded and, with a courtly half-bow that belonged to another century, he too left the library.

When Herrera was sure he was unobserved, he opened the French doors and walked outside, his normally pleasant features marred by a frown.

Crewe's employer intercepted him on the path to the jetty where the launch was waiting.

"You realize how important Donovan's information could be to us?"

"Yes, *señor*. Don't worry, Donovan and I have this understanding. If he knows anything, he'll tell me."

"Unless the girl has played on his sympathies, in which

case he may not wish us to know anything. If he seems . . . reticent, I trust you will persuade him to cooperate?"

Crewe's heavy brow wrinkled, as though he were perplexed by the three-syllable words, then he grinned and nodded. "Gotcha. Whatever he knows, I'll know."

— 4 —

"You *lost* it?" Felix's voice held the exact mixture of incredulity and anger that Donovan had expected. "You *lost* twenty-five hundred dollars? You *lost* the entire month's profit?" His brown eyes, widened in shocked amazement, locked on his partner's face and seemed to dare Donovan to find an excuse for himself.

Donovan didn't even try. In the five years they'd worked together, Donovan had learned that anger affected Felix's hearing; he became deaf until the rage had passed. So Donovan resigned himself to the gestures, the pacing, and the cursing, the latter of which quickly became more colorful, even unique, as it slid from English into Spanish. Felix's fluency in his mother language hadn't been dulled by twenty years in the States.

"We haven't even paid for the parts you put into that bucket last month! Juliana quit this morning because I'm over a week late with her paycheck, and she's holding the accounts for ransom! Do you see this? *This* is a letter from the oil company! It says we have ten days, exactly ten days, to pay the account in full or they'll revoke our credit! And *you* have *lost* the money?"

Donovan perched on the battered desk that adorned the center of the small room and contemplated the olive-drab filing cabinet standing sentinel beside the door. For the first time since he'd quit smoking several weeks earlier, he truly craved a cigarette. It wasn't the niggling little prick of irritation he'd suffered through at first, when he would reach for the pack of Camels that wasn't there anymore. It was a full-blown, horrendous hunger. He found himself glancing around the cramped, paper-strewn office for one of Felix's foul-smelling *cigarillos* and instantly banished the impulse—he hated those things.

Then he realized Felix had stopped shouting. "Are you through?"

"Only for the next five minutes while you explain." Felix flexed his broad shoulders as though trying to ease an incipient spasm. "And it better be good, old buddy. You were supposed to finish up with Crewe last night in plenty of time to get back here for the charter this morning. At nine-thirty I get a call from Lopez—you didn't show up. Now it's three in the afternoon. Not only did we lose Lopez, you tell me everything else is gone too. Jay, what the hell happened?"

"I ran into a little trouble. The money was stolen . . ."

"At least you put up a good fight, judging from your face. Do you need to see a doctor?"

"No, I'm okay. She just caught me off guard. I got sloppy." A surge of hard, cold anger sent his arm sweeping across the haphazard stacks of papers on the desk. "Damn it, how could I have let this happen!"

"She? You were ripped off by a woman?" Felix looked as though he didn't know whether to laugh or cry. Donovan didn't blame him—it was hard for him to believe, and he'd *been* there.

He pinched the bridge of his nose between thumb and forefinger, fervently wishing he'd put off this particular chore. He couldn't remember ever having been this tired. "Just call her Hurricane Anna."

"Incredible," Felix muttered, shaking his head. "Absolutely incredible." He crossed the room to rummage through a cabinet behind the desk. "Wet your throat, *amigo*," he said, passing a pint bottle to Donovan. "You've got a lot of talking to do, and I don't want you to dry up before you're finished."

Donovan could have done without the talking, but he accepted the bottle with relish. The liquor burned going down, reminding him how long it had been since he'd had a drink. This was too much to expect of anyone; on his way home he was going to give in to his baser instincts and buy five packs of Camels and a fifth of whatever was cheapest. No, he wouldn't. He couldn't. He didn't have any money.

"She said her name was Anna," he began. "I picked her up early this morning on Sonrisa . . ."

Anna looked out the window of the plane. The sunlight glinted off the wing, hurting her eyes. She closed her lids wearily and sighed.

It had been close, so close. The queasiness of fear still hadn't left her. After her frantic flight and desperate scrabbling to escape the island, she'd nearly walked headlong into their trap. The memory unnerved her, and she clasped her hands together to still their trembling.

They'd been watching the ticket counters, two of them, both stamped with that indefinable air of furtive danger she'd noticed through the years in so many of her grandfather's acquaintances. She didn't kid herself that she spotted them because of her alertness; she'd been too tired, too upset over what had happened back in the hotel room. No, it was pure luck that she had glanced toward the gift shop and seen the man browsing through the paperback books. When she'd withdrawn a few safe paces before he'd had a chance to spot her, she'd seen the other one lounging against the wall, ostensibly waiting for a debarking passenger.

Her shaking legs had carried her to the ladies' room, and ten minutes later she'd emerged a different Anna, dressed in new clothes, a somewhat out-of-date turban to cover her hair, and skillfully applied makeup that subtly changed the shape of her mouth, the contours of her cheeks. With the addition of sunglasses, she felt reasonably confident of getting past the watchdogs unnoticed.

Thank God for the Latin temperament, she thought. In the States it wouldn't have been so easy to enlist the aid of two fellow travelers to make her purchases and pretend to be her companions. The young women had been both thrilled and impressed to be included in something so exciting as an elopement.

She'd made her flight with only minutes to spare, expecting to be stopped with every step.

"*Señorita?*"

Anna looked up at the smiling stewardess with the cart of tiny bottles and declined the drink with a shake of her head.

The first hurdle was past; now she had to hope that Wynette got her message and would be at LAX to meet her flight. Once 'Tavio was certain she was no longer in Santa Marta, Los Angeles would be the next place he'd check— her apartment, the campus, her friends. Except for Wynette. She had no recent connection with Anna's job as a high school counselor and none at all with the campus where Anna took postgraduate courses two nights a week. She would be safe staying with Wynette for a while, at least until she could decide what to do.

Once again she looked out the window at the blue-green expanse of ocean that stretched away to the west. She wondered what was happening on Sonrisa, what 'Tavio was doing now, at this moment. She wondered how she could ever explain to Wynette, or if she should even try. She wondered about Donovan and wished she hadn't.

Because in her terror he was the one she wanted beside her, and she didn't know why, any more than she knew why she'd made love with him the night before. He was a stranger, someone she didn't trust. But she actually missed him—she *needed* him. A memory from their hour on the beach brushed her mind, then took hold. She could almost feel his fingers brushing away her tears, and inside her something stirred.

She thought she must be going crazy.

*   *   *

Donovan climbed the stairs behind Raoul's Bar to the low-rent cubbyhole he wished he didn't call home. The rusty lock on the paint-poor apartment door resisted his key with determination. Calling upon his severely depleted reserves of coordination, he at last turned the tumblers and the door swung open into a square room not much larger than the Huey's cockpit. A fifty-watt bulb dangled from a black cord in the approximate center of the ceiling; as usual, Donovan wished he didn't have to switch it on. Living here was bad enough—seeing it sometimes aggravated his embryonic ulcer.

He safely maneuvered around the brownish early-Depression divan, then cursed when he stumbled against the three-legged table propped in the corner next to his bed. Those two shots of Felix's rotgut had proved dangerous to a man in Donovan's condition, and he was glad his common sense had talked him out of having more. He comforted himself with the reflection that Felix, after killing the bottle, was now in much worse shape than his partner, in spite of a full belly and plenty of sleep the night before.

The cot, with its pitiful mattress and limp springs, had never looked more inviting, but he couldn't allow himself the luxury of sleep, not yet. There was still the problem of Anna-what's-her-name and his twenty-five hundred dollars.

Over a stained sink in the makeshift bathroom he splashed tepid water on his battered face and gingerly felt his nose. It appeared to be slightly askew, but he wouldn't be able to tell for sure until the swelling went down. He should, he supposed, be grateful she hadn't knocked out a couple of teeth, but gratitude seemed to elude him. His overriding concern at the moment was that she had ripped off his money, his ID, and Felix's credit card. She'd also made a fool of him, which hurt considerably worse than his nose. And he didn't even have the satisfaction of knowing what it was all about.

Felix, damn his black eyes, had been no help, though he'd said he could make some inquiries in a few back rooms. Once the shock had worn off, he'd actually found the episode amusing—at Donovan's expense, of course. But then, Felix didn't understand.

That skinny, sad-eyed female was lethal, a walking menace—in more ways than one. Would her deceptively helpless look have fooled him if he'd never touched her softness? Would he have been more guarded if he'd never held her in his arms? He didn't know, but the possibility existed, and that in itself was a tough admission to make.

Donovan allowed himself to acknowledge only two types of women—the ones he paid and the ones he didn't want. The strategy had worked well up until now. But Anna, with her crooked nose, her jet-set poise, and her incredible sensuality, had thrown him, literally and figuratively. She was the worst thing that could have happened to him.

Carefully skirting the wobbly table, he crossed the room to open the midget refrigerator and glumly surveyed its contents, thinking that real food might help to offset the effects of the alcohol. He had to settle for a suspicious-looking piece of cheese slapped between two slices of stale bread. He bit into the sandwich and grimaced. The taste suggested something he'd rather not think about, and his stomach wouldn't appreciate it in the least.

He spit the bite into the cardboard box that served as a trash can and dropped the sandwich in after it. He'd bet Miss Anna had never had to worry about an empty refrigerator. No one would ever mistake her thinness for malnutrition. She was class, all the way down to her skinny toes. Something had her worried, though; it had her scared to death.

In the parlor cum kitchen cum bedroom, he lay his protesting body on the sagging cot and closed his eyes, trying to ignore the steady boom-boom of the juke box coming from the bar directly beneath him.

The lady's problem could be something as uncomplicated as a jealous husband, maybe even an angry pimp. But he didn't think so. He had a hunch it concerned old Michelotti. If the rumors were anywhere close to the truth, Sonrisa had been the home base for a crime syndicate for close to half a century. And a day after the kingpin's death, a woman was running scared, fighting and stealing to get away. Coincidence? Donovan didn't believe in it.

Maybe she knew something about the old man's death. Maybe she'd been *involved* in his death.

Donovan discarded that half-formed notion with disturbing insight. Somehow he knew she was incapable of murder. If he were to be honest with himself, he seemed to know a lot about her that he shouldn't.

Without warning, a flash from the night before shocked him with its intensity. When he'd cupped her face in his hands, he'd known how her skin would feel beneath his fingers. He'd known how to touch her, where to kiss her. There'd been no fumbling, no awkwardness or hesitation. They had fit together like two halves of a whole. The realization frightened him.

He didn't want this—he certainly didn't need it. He wanted to forget about her *and* her problem, whatever it was; he wanted to tell himself the little hellion was capable of handling anything or anyone who crossed her path. But as surely as he knew his name, he knew Anna. *She's not tough*, he admitted, *just desperate*.

He flopped onto his side and winced as his bruised ribs came into sharp contact with a displaced spring. He should be angry, seething with resentment, but he just couldn't seem to work himself up to it. The fact annoyed him more than just a little.

And as though he needed further agitation, a tiny impression that had been lurking in the background decided to make itself more fully felt: he wanted to *do* something, come to her rescue, save her from the bad guys, whoever they were. But where would he start? He didn't even know her last name.

For the first time in nearly fifteen years, Donovan was actually worried about someone other than himself. It was a sobering situation, and he wore it uncomfortably for several minutes. Then the feeling settled in, and he found himself hoping the twenty-five hundred would be enough to take her to safety.

His thoughts amused him, and he grinned at the fly-specked ceiling. "You're getting old, Irish," he said into the shabby room, "old and slipshod and soft. Maybe it's time to go back to Indiana, raise hogs and age gracefully." He chuckled at the image. There had been nothing particularly graceful about his departure from the family farm twenty-three years ago; if he showed up now, the old man would probably greet him with a shotgun.

When he caught himself wondering what Anna would think about slopping hogs and going to stock auctions, his amusement vanished. She was rapidly becoming an obsession, and he was too exhausted to deal with it on any sane level.

He had to get some rest. Felix had promised to drop by later with whatever information he could ferret out so they could discuss a game plan, and Donovan thought he'd better be able to pay attention. He considered getting undressed but the effort seemed too great. He'd sleep for a few hours, then get up and shower. . . .

Someone was pounding on the door, an angry and insistent racket. Undoubtedly it was Felix, and he didn't seem to be in the best of moods.

Donovan had barely rolled to his feet when the tone and rhythm of the noise changed abruptly. The door flew open, spraying slivers of wood, and a very large man stumbled in, following the impetus of his shoulder. Flanking him were two other men, one equally large.

The third was a familiar figure, short, stocky, still clad in the incongruous gray suit. Crewe.

Donovan's drowsiness vanished immediately. His common sense, abetted by the whirlpool in the middle of his small intestine, told him the reason for Crewe's visit. Anna. Whatever decision he made would have to be made now. He could talk to them and they'd probably go away. He could try to fight them and probably get killed. He could play stupid and possibly get no worse than a beating.

He compromised and opted for the possible.

"Nice of you to drop in, Crewe. Did you decide to give me another bonus?"

Crewe's sneer was top-notch nasty. He'd obviously been practicing.

"I expected something a little classier from you, Ace." His porcine eyes, firmly set in their fleshy sockets, roamed around the room, prying out every shabbiness from every corner. "You know, plush carpets, a bar, that sorta stuff."

Donovan reached for the pack of Camels on the three-legged table. It was empty.

"Well, gee, guys, you should have let me know you were coming. I'd have cleaned up the place."

The big boys moved in a step or two, clearly unamused. Donovan was surprised by their stereotypically stupid villainy—big, mechanical hulks with no other purpose than to obey orders. He'd thought that type existed only in the movies.

"C'mon, Ace, don't try to be cute. We just need a little information, then we'll get out of your hair. Where's the girl?"

Donovan looked disapproving. "Girl? You came to the wrong place for that kind of thing, boys. I run a clean business . . ."

One of the hulks moved a step closer and Donovan tensed. He knew what was coming—it was inevitable. He couldn't give Crewe what he wanted; there was no way out of the apartment, not even a window; he couldn't take on both of Crewe's playmates. Nobody in the bar downstairs would hear anything that happened, and wouldn't care if they did. And he figured his odds against bluffing it out were about a million to one.

"Give us both a break, Ace." Under the circumstances,

Donovan thought, Crewe was showing an amazing degree of tolerance. "The lady's important to a very big man; he's worried about her. You can understand that, can't you? Now, where is she?"

Donovan decided to press his luck a little further. "We're missing a couple of ingredients here, Crewe. One, who are we talking about? Two, why am I supposed to have her?"

"Two strikes and one to go. This is your last chance, Ace."

Donovan threw up his hands in a placating gesture. "Okay, okay. Yeah, I picked up this broad on the island. She said she wanted to go to Guaymas, so I said, why not? What's the big deal?"

"Like I said, she's a very important little lady. The Family's worried about her. Where is she?"

"What's with you, Crewe? I just told you, she flew back to Guaymas with me. I didn't see her again after we landed. Hell, she didn't even tell me her name."

"I like you, Donovan. But I think you're lyin'. And I have to ask myself, why? I mean, we've always had a good working relationship; why spoil it now?"

Donovan tried to prepare himself for the assault. Crewe had the look of a hungry man intent on feasting. "Sorry I can't help you . . ."

A fist, ham huge and brick hard, slammed into his stomach. He doubled over, gasping for air and trying not to vomit.

Crewe's voice sounded again. It seemed to be farther away but it was still unpleasant. "You're bein' cute, Donovan. The boys don't like it when you're cute. Now, the way I see it, you're in a no-win situation here. All we want to know is where you took the girl."

"I'd really like to help you, Crewe, especially since your friends seem to be so touchy." Donovan's insides felt like mush, and he had a feeling things were going to get worse before they got better. But when he thought of telling them what they wanted to know, his tongue seemed to wiggle away from the words. "But I can't tell you what I don't know. She got out of the chopper at the airstrip. She left. I don't know where she is . . ."

A set of fingers gripped his hair, yanking his head back viciously. He heard his neck pop. Then the fist hit his midsection again. When he doubled up this time, he fell, hard, onto the linoleum floor. A well-aimed foot caught him in the kidneys. After the first burst of agony, he welcomed the fog that surrounded his mind, protecting him. It was almost as good as the *bruma* . . .

From a couple of light-years away, he could still hear Crewe's voice, nasal and rough. "No need to go overboard, Joey. Ease up."

"But you said·you wanted him to talk . . ."

"Does he look like he's talking, monkey-brain? We gotta find the Michellotti broad and make sure her mouth's shut for good, and he can't tell us if he's dead."

Donovan focused on the name and struggled to hang on to consciousness. Michelotti. Her name was Anna Michelotti, and these cretins wanted her. Why?

He felt the hands, cruel and impatient, that gripped·his upper arms and hauled him to his feet, but the pain was negligible compared with the agony that flared throughout the rest of his body.

"C'mon, buddy, don't be so hard-nosed. We know you took her off the island. What's in it for you, anyway? You think she's waiting for you somewhere so you can live happily ever after? Wise up, Donovan." Crewe's voice sounded weary now. "There's no percentage in being the good guy."

Donovan heard another voice, weak but familiar—his own?—saying, "Shove it . . ."

Then the world exploded and he went to hell, hurting every inch of the way.

By seven o'clock dusk had settled firmly over Los Angeles, leaving a false sense of serenity over the city and an ache in Anna's heart.

She stood at the bedroom window, looking at nothing in

particular, clutching Wynette's too-long terry robe across her breasts. A long shower had refreshed her body but not her spirit, and she was feeling more and more dejected. Not only had she not come up with any course of action, but Donovan refused to be banished from her thoughts.

She looked at the wallet lying on the bed, in which she'd found his identification. Most of the money was still there, and she could easily replace what she'd had to spend; then she could mail it back to him, proving she was no thief. And in spite of the blood on his face, she felt reasonably confident that she had done him no lasting damage.

On a more intimate level, she felt that the episode on the beach was, when measured against everything else assailing her life at the moment, of little importance. After all, things like that happened all the time—just because they'd never happened to her before was no reason to exaggerate the importance of that one interlude. In her grief and need, she'd reached out and he'd reached back, each of them finding a measure of comfort and fulfillment. Anything deeper or more meaningful than that was only a figment of her overactive imagination.

There was no good reason for this man to occupy so much of her mental space, but she couldn't seem to get rid of him. She couldn't even put a name to what she felt, and that was the most aggravating thing of all.

"Hey!" Wynette's voice called from the other room. "Are you gonna stay in there all night? You owe me an explanation, remember?"

Anna winced. She did indeed owe her friend an explanation, but she hadn't the slightest idea what she should say. Wynette was, of course, confused; during the trip from the airport, Anna had been noncommittal, saying nothing to answer Wynette's numerous questions. Only a promise to explain it all later had kept her curiosity at bay. Now it was time to pay up.

The bedroom door opened, and Wynette's café au lait face, undeniably lovely even without her elaborate makeup, made an appearance. "Did you hear me, girl? Get on in here, put a drink in your hand, and start talkin'."

"Okay," Anna laughed. Though she was the older by eight years, Wynette had always called her "girl." There were even times when Wynette's wisdom and straight-on logic made Anna feel almost immature by comparison. But she didn't mind; she'd never had a truer friend or one to whom she felt closer. "Who's tending bar?"

"Yours truly," Wynette answered, leading the way into the living room. "Nobody can open a bottle like me."

She handed Anna a tall glass of something fruity, and they both sank into the navy blue plush sofa that dominated the center of the large room. Anna, looking at the understated elegance of her surroundings, marveled at the change in Wynette's lifestyle and character. Five years ago she'd been an angry, defiant fifteen-year-old who spent more time on the streets than at home or in school. Now she was well on her way to success as a model, and the bud of promise Anna had sensed so long ago had now blossomed into a beautiful warmth and grace.

"Now," Wynette said, bringing her back to the present, "you can start with why you showed up scared to death, with no luggage and painted up like Friday night on the Strip. And then that sprint through the airport, knockin' people over. You're actin' *strange*, girl."

"I know." Anna sipped the drink, swallowed it gratefully. "You deserve an explanation, Wyn, but I'm not going to give it to you, not now. I shouldn't even have called you, because it's not fair to involve you in this. But I just didn't know what else to do."

Wynette looked at her friend searchingly, her young face troubled. "This is really serious, isn't it? I mean, more than your grandfather's death and the funeral?"

Anna nodded. "Deadly serious. And the less you know about it, the better. I'm in trouble, Wyn, and it could touch the people around me."

Wynette's eyes, large and almond shaped, had grown

almost round with apprehension. "If you're tryin' to scare me, Anna girl, you're doin' a good job." Her drink sat forgotten on the small, glass-topped table beside the sofa. "But you helped me when I needed it most, when there wasn't a soul in this world willin' to give me another chance. So as far as I'm concerned, your trouble is my trouble and I want to help if I can. That business back at the airport—you were afraid of being seen, weren't you?"

Anna nodded. "I need to stay out of sight for a while, away from my apartment and the campus."

"What about work?"

"They're not expecting me back until Tuesday, and I shouldn't have any trouble getting more time off. I've got plenty of vacation and sick leave coming."

"Well, if all you need is a parking space, I've got just the thing," Wynette told her, smiling. "You're lookin' at the proud owner of a new condo. It's right on the beach, the very finest in *dee*-luxe accommodations. How does that sound?"

Anna thought it sounded tailor-made. "Where?"

"Laguna Beach. We just closed on it last week, and I was planning to go down next weekend anyway. We'll just go several days early."

"The place sounds great, Wyn, but I don't like the idea of us being seen together. You just don't know how serious this really is."

"Okay, so you take the car and go on ahead. You can leave Monday and I'll wait 'til Friday."

"But I'll have your car . . ."

"No problem. I'll rent one. Anything else?"

Anna laughed. "I guess not. When did you become Ms. Take Charge?"

They settled into easy talk. Anna curled her legs up beneath her and leaned her head back. The next thing she knew, Wyn was gently shaking her awake.

"C'mon, girl," Wynette said softly, "time to get you in bed. And don't worry about gettin' up in the mornin'. It's Sunday and you can sleep all day."

Anna felt slightly ridiculous, being tucked into bed like a child, but not ridiculous enough to protest. It felt good to be taken care of. For a moment she longed desperately to be a little girl again, surrounded by Poppy's authority and love, with no bigger problem than finding a lost puppy. Then she took hold of the self-pity and shook it away. She was a big girl now, intelligent and capable of dealing with her problems, even this one. Poppy would expect no less of her, and she should expect no less of herself.

But when sleep finally claimed her, she dreamed of Sonrisa and butterflies and flowers, and for a while she was happy again.

The man in the car parked across the street from Wynette's apartment house glanced at his watch. She'd been in there for several hours, and he thought it unlikely that she'd come out again tonight. He would go home, get a good night's rest and take up the vigil again the next morning.

As he drove through the narrow streets of the fashionable Los Angeles suburb, he wondered again who the woman was and why she'd been targeted by his contact. He had a bad feeling about this job and wished, as he had several times since the phone call, that he could have refused it. But a marker had been called in, an important favor he'd nearly forgotten over the years, and the man he owed was too important—and too dangerous—to cross.

If only he hadn't spotted her at the airport, his part would be over now and he wouldn't be fighting the creepy feeling that he was involved in a very nasty business.

Her friend, too, was another stroke of luck, depending on your point of view. Very visible, very noticeable. He'd thought she looked familiar, and after dredging through his considerable memory, he recognized her from several recent magazine ads and television commercials.

Neither of them seemed the sort to be mixed up with the man from Mexico. Of course, neither had he eight years ago. Maybe the woman was going to get exactly what she deserved. But he doubted it. He just wanted to call in his report and get out of the whole mess.

He had a hunch, though, that his part wasn't yet done, and the suspicion left him feeling sick.

5

AN EXPLOSION ROCKED the deuce-and-a-half, lighting the night with an obscene burst of fireworks. He fought the wheel for control and prayed desperately to any god who might be listening to let him make just another mile, just five thousand feet more, just let him find them safe and whole and then he didn't care what happened to him, just keep them safe, his woman and his son, please, God, please let them be all right and whole and he'd never ask for anything again, just don't take them away . . .

Another mortar round, then another, almost on top of him, shook the truck viciously. He imagined that he could hear shell fragments ripping into the truck even through the deafening battle thunder. His luck had held so far; the radiator hadn't been pierced, and the windshield wasn't yet so badly pitted that he couldn't see. But how much farther could he make it? Another three-quarters of a mile, that's all he needed, a lousy three-quarters of a mile.

Directly ahead the high beams picked out a figure in the road, dark pants and tunic fading into the surrounding night. He laid on the horn. The figure turned; a round hit twenty yards to the right. Like a rag doll flung by a careless hand, the figure flew several feet, then lay crumpled and still.

Automatically he braked, though his mind kept repeating, No time, no time. Mechanically he opened the door, stepped out, examined the old man by the dim flare of a cigarette lighter. A piece of shrapnel protruded from the base of the skull.

A shell exploded ahead of him. In a crouch, he began running the few steps to the truck. Before he reached the cab, another round went off and he fell, clutching his leg, trying to squeeze the *agonizing pain away. Somehow he regained his feet, refusing to think about the knee that must surely be shattered, concentrating only on resuming his journey.*

Through sheer exertion of will, he regained his seat in the cab, though he was weak with pain and wet with perspiration. The truck began its sway-and-lurch journey again, quickly gaining speed. The right front tire hit a crater, and he bounced forward against the steering wheel, splitting the skin high on his cheekbone. Blood mingled with the tears running down his face, and he angrily slapped away the moisture.

The concussion from another explosion buffeted the truck, but less fiercely this time, farther behind him. He was almost through. A quarter of a mile would see him there. He chose to take it as a sign—he wouldn't have made it this far if he wasn't going to make it all the way. They were waiting for him; she'd promised to wait until he came to lead them to safety. "I will be here, Dahno-Vahn," she'd said; "we will both be here. You worry too much." And she'd laughed.

But when the fighting shifted to the north while he was on his last mission, there'd been no way to get word to her, to tell her to leave with the other evacuees. She would be there, waiting. She'd promised, and she never broke her word.

He bounced around a curve, and the headlights picked out the forms of several huts. As he drew nearer, his gut tightened. Only a few of the structures were whole. The rest were flattened, burned. He opened the door and hit the ground in a run. His own footsteps were the only sound he heard.

He shouted her name.

He screamed her name.

He found her where she'd said she would be, in her own home, waiting for him with the baby in her arms. Her brown eyes seemed to watch him as he knelt, touched her face, took his son from her arms. She couldn't see him, of course, but he felt her eyes on him anyway. Just as he heard her soft voice saying, "I waited for you, Dahno-Vahn. I waited . . ."

"*. . . you think she's waiting for you somewhere? . . .*"

He knew the voice, hated it, tried to shut it out.

62

". . .wise up, Donovan . . ."
Why didn't he shut up, go away?
". . . you think she's waiting . . ."
Waiting, she's waiting . . .

"Hey, buddy, say something. I'm getting lonesome."

Donovan opened his eyes slowly, feeling that anything done quickly would intensify the half dozen pockets of torturous pain deposited at every strategic point of his anatomy. Felix's face hovered above him for a moment, then wavered. Donovan gave up the effort and closed his eyes again.

"It's about time," Felix said. "I hate to admit it, but I was getting worried about you."

"What did you do, break up the party?" God, even his throat hurt.

"Me and a few guys from the bar downstairs. But not soon enough, I think. What the hell's going on?"

"I guess you could say I was being interrogated." He wanted to cough but was afraid to. "What time is it anyway?"

"For you, the next day. You've been out nearly fourteen hours."

Donovan raised his eyelids carefully and peered around the room through lashes that felt like cement. The sterile, white walls glared at him. "So what's the prognosis?"

Felix shrugged. "The doc said you didn't have any head injuries, just plenty of sore spots. You can leave today if you feel like it." He perched on the foot of the hospital bed and took out a *cigarillo*. "What happened, Jay? From what I saw, those goons were trying to kill you."

"Just a friendly interrogation." Donovan moved his left arm and groaned. "They thought I had something that belonged to them."

"Knock it off, buddy." Felix sounded angry. "I already know some of it; you may as well tell me the rest."

Donovan looked at him sharply. "What do you know?"

Felix considered for a moment before answering.

Though his words were casual, there was an odd tension in his voice. "Old Michelotti had a granddaughter. She disappeared early yesterday morning." Felix rolled the *cigarillo* around on his tongue. "Today the streets are crawling with 'interrogators'. Seems the little lady's fiancé is worried about her."

"Fiancé?" The concept was startling, but no more so than the flood of possessiveness that swept through him. "Who?"

"Octavio Herrera. He was Michelotti's right hand for years. Now that the old man's dead, it looks like he's the top hand."

"I'm impressed." He was annoyed.

"You should be. The guys who did a number on you work for said fiancé." Felix's dark eyes were unexpectedly grim. "I'm pretty good with numbers, amigo, and the way I add it up, you've got big trouble."

It took a moment or two for the implications to connect in Donovan's still-sluggish thought processes, but when they did, his stomach turned over.

"Not me." He felt old and useless and scared. "Her. Anna. They just wanted me to tell them where she is. It's her they want to kill."

The weather was inappropriately nice. Anna thought there should, at the very least, be one hell of a storm whipping everything around. That's how she felt, like she'd been whipped by a storm. For all the sleep she'd gotten the night before, she'd have done better to simply stay up. Twice she'd dozed off, only to be jerked awake by nightmares she couldn't remember.

Now here she was, cruising through Southern California in a Firebird convertible, on her way to a fancy condominium on the beach. Just like a tourist, for Pete's sake. Just like nothing had ever happened.

Saturday she'd thought if she could just get back to L.A., everything would be all right, the answers to the problems would appear like magic. Well, she was here, but the answers were as elusive as ever. Things looked even worse than they had two days ago, if that were possible. Now, just by being here, she'd involved Wynette; how could she undo that? How could she protect herself?

The telephone conversation she'd heard came rushing back to her, the words producing the same feelings of shock and horror as they had the first time . . .

We lost the last shipment in the desert . . . I agree, it was unnecessary, but death is unavoidable in our business . . . a result of poor planning and poor supervision. Next time I will attend to the details personally . . . lost a great deal of money, but it can be replaced. Herrera has been financing the operation for two years . . . he will have access to even more through Don Roberto's granddaughter . . .

In spite of the warmth of the October sun, she was cold; she shivered in the strong breeze blowing through the open car. She'd been gripping the steering wheel with fingers held rigidly tense. Now she flexed her right hand to relieve a cramp, drew in a shaky breath. While the golden California landscape swept past, Anna tried once again, as she had so often during the past thirty-six hours, to make some sense of it all.

Why would 'Tavio be a part of something so horrible? He'd always known that Poppy intended to leave him a sizeable bequest and, of course, he would have shared her inheritance once they were married. It didn't make sense that he was in it for the money. Blackmail? A connection from his past? He'd been a street kid, doing whatever he could to survive when Poppy had found him, but he'd lived on Sonrisa as Poppy's protégé since he was fifteen. Could he have been secretly working with his old friends for over twenty years?

Oh, stop it, Anna! she told herself fiercely. There was no way of figuring it out now, and it didn't matter anyway. His involvement was the only relevant fact; his betrayal, both of herself and Poppy, proved how blind love could be.

Not that she'd been in love with him, but she had cared enough to agree to marry him, as Poppy had wished. 'Tavio had been her friend, her confidante, and she mourned his loss.

She had to stop thinking about it, had to get her mind on something else before she turned into a basket case. If she kept spinning at this pace, she'd be useless, fit for nothing except hiding in Laguna Beach for the rest of her life.

She reached for the radio knob, flicked it on. The perfectly balanced speakers released a flood of music that swept past her to float away on the California breeze—Bob Seger singing about brave strangers. The driving rhythm boomed through her head, the words invoking Donovan and the taste of his kisses. They also brought an aching reget. Anna felt suddenly that their meeting had been orchestrated by an unseen hand, a puppeteer working the strings of their lives. It had been incredible, the pull between them. She'd lain in his arms, shared a depth of emotion she'd only guessed at before, yet neither of them had spoken.

Would he think of her in years to come, remember his "brave stranger" of the beach? Or would he remember only the woman who'd lied to him, stolen from him?

The words of the song insisted it would be all right.

But it wouldn't be all right. Donovan was lost to her before she even knew she had found him. The question of his association with 'Tavio was no longer important, only her need and aching loneliness. Donovan's brief touch had somehow changed her, made her more than she'd ever been.

Her eyes burning with tears she refused to shed, Anna turned off the radio and tried to force him from her mind. She had to stop thinking about him before she drove herself crazy with regret and longing. She'd mail the wallet to him today, right now, then it would be finished.

The decision seemed to bring her a measure of peace.

Laguna Beach was quiet and attractive, the kind of town

that bespoke lots of money and an aloofness that repelled the "rowdy element." There were lots of expensive shops and exclusive restaurants, plenty of Caddies and Lincolns. As she drove around searching for the post office, she saw tawny, elegant-looking women coming and going, obviously affluent men in three-piece suits entering the restaurants for lunch. There wasn't a pickup or Volkswagen or gang of kids in sight. It was hard for her to imagine Wynette in this atmosphere; her young friend must have been looking for status rather than roots when she took the condo.

She pulled into a service station to ask directions to the post office, and a tall young man with lots of white teeth bounded out to greet her.

"Hey, how's it going? Need some unleaded?"

She'd have bet a month's pay that he worked as a lifeguard during the summer and spent his days off riding the waves on his new sailboard. "No gas, thanks. Where's the post office here?"

"Right up the street there, you can't miss it." He eyed the Firebird with youthful hunger. "Narley car."

Anna laughed. "Thanks." It would probably be a couple of years yet, she thought, before the gleam in his eye glowed brighter for a female than for a convertible. "Maybe next time I'll let you wash and wax it for me."

"Hey, thanks!" He couldn't have been more thrilled if she'd given him a ten-dollar tip. As she drove away, Anna waved and smiled, missing her lost youth and carefree enthusiasm. *I didn't feel this old yesterday*, she thought sadly.

The post office was right where the young man had said it would be. The woman behind the counter wasn't quite as friendly as the station attendant, but she did consent to find a small box and some strapping tape. Anna wrote a short note and slipped it in with the bills, then wrapped the wallet slowly, somehow reluctant to let it go. For the first time she tried to honestly appraise her action. Was she really trying to assuage her guilt, or did she want to remind him of her existence? When she gave the parcel to the clerk, her fingers tightened around it for a moment. Was she breaking a link or forging one?

She found Wynette's condominium easily, sighing with relief as she turned into the driveway. For the past ten minutes, ever since leaving the post office, she'd been growing more and more uneasy. Twice she'd noticed a blue sedan behind her, never too close, and it had passed her when she slowed down. But the feeling persisted. *It's just nerves, stop worrying*, she told herself. Still, she sat in the car for a while, looking at the street, before she got out and walked up the drive.

The condominiums were relatively new with a sleek, modern exterior, a large pool around which four or five people were lounging, and a magnificent ocean frontage. The first-story front windows all faced the beach, and each apartment was graced with a small, railed, second-story balcony. Beyond the building, the ocean rolled in on gentle breakers that whispered a soft, gentle lullaby, a melody that reminded her of Sonrisa, a song of home.

Anna checked the key Wynette had given her and matched the number to one of the doors along the sidewalk. As she passed the pool, she was aware of the curious glances from the group of loungers and wondered if she looked as conspicuous as she felt. Fitting key to lock, she turned the tumblers and gratefully entered the cool, darkened foyer. Inside, the large rooms lived up to the outside promise. The kitchen was separated from the living area by a long, blue-topped counter, and the cream walls caught the light from the floor-to-ceiling windows and bounced it into every corner. Wynette had obviously just begun decorating, for there were only a few pieces of furniture: a chair and love seat of heavy, dark cane with polished-cotton cushions, a low oriental table, and three oversized floor pillows. A smaller alcove off the kitchen, obviously for dining, was completely bare except for an excellent watercolor that adorned the wall. Upstairs, the bedrooms carried through with the uncluttered theme. Both had platform beds and little else, but the one with the balcony overlooked the water. In that room she dropped her bag and stretched out across the bed.

Anna felt the knots loosening inside her, and the sudden release made her feel almost too tired to take another step. The first thing she wanted to do was take a nap, a long one; then she'd go walking. Maybe tomorrow she would call 'Tavio, spin out her story. But for now she wanted only to rest.

Much later, as she walked the dark, deserted beach, it occurred to her that she'd made at least one decision, even if she hadn't known it at the time—she'd decided Donovan wasn't one of the bad guys.

He liked it less and less. Instinct told him this was a dirty job, one he'd be ashamed of if he knew the whole story. If he had the guts, he'd walk away from it now before he became any more involved. But the man in Mexico had a long arm, and a deadly one.

The woman had gone into the condo several hours ago with only a small bag. Either she didn't plan to stay long or she travelled light. Just in case it was the former, he thought it would be safer to stick around and make sure she was tucked in. Later he would call in his report and hope he'd be let off the hook. She looked like a decent person. Even the kid at the service station, to whom she'd spoken only a few words, described her as "real. A lady, you know?" He wondered again what kind of threat she could be to the man in Mexico.

She looked a little bit like his ex-wife, Jeannie. The same long legs and thin face, the same way of tossing her hair back out of the way. She even walked like Jeannie, with that easy kind of move that reminded you of dancing.

A spasm twisted his stomach, and he reached for the antacid pills he always carried with him. He wondered if his body was trying to tell him the same thing his conscience was. This was wrong, all wrong. He'd had to do a lot of dirty things during his life, but he didn't think he'd ever been responsible for the destruction of an innocent human being. And she was innocent. He knew that from an instinct born of working with the other kind for too many years.

He chewed the tablets slowly, turning over the burgeoning decision in his mind. He would do it. He'd play the game until time for his next report, then he would lie to the man in Mexico. He'd let the girl off the hook, and himself too. It was time, and past, for a change.

And when he was out for good, he'd find Jeannie. It was time, and past, for that too.

Three days later, Donovan sat behind the desk in the cramped, dusty office going through the pile of overdue statements Felix had saddled him with, fighting a wholehearted desire to dump the lot in the wastebasket and start a bonfire. Somewhere in the universe, he was sure, there existed a task he hated more than the one in hand, but for the moment he couldn't imagine what it might be. He was totally useless indoors, almost claustrophobic. He didn't know how he would get through the next few days until he could fly again.

Besides, he didn't have room for thoughts of anything except Anna Michelotti. Most of his energy seemed to be used up thinking about her, worrying about her, trying to work out the puzzle. Why would Herrera want to kill her? What had happened that night between 2 A.M. and dawn?

It had to have been sudden and unexpected; he was sure of it. When she'd been with him, she was upset but not frantic, not running for her life. She must have seen or heard something after she left him, something that not only frightened her but made her a potential liability to Herrera. Herrera's solution? Do whatever it took to silence her.

Now it was too late for Donovan to help her. He had no

inkling where she might have gone. If Crewe had bought his story about bringing her to Guaymas, then she'd had time to get out of the country, but it was possible she was still holed up in Santa Marta. It wasn't too likely that she had any experience in disappearing, so there was an outside chance he could track her down if she was still in town. He mentally sifted through his contacts, picking several who might be able to ferret out some information for him.

Felix elbowed his way through the door, carrying a double handful of mail, a small, brown package balanced atop the letters. "You straightened out that mess yet?" he asked, dropping the mail on the desk.

"Sure," Donovan said. "We don't pay any of them, they throw us in jail, and we both get free room and board for the next five years."

"Sounds reasonable." Felix shuffled through the envelopes, tossed several toward Donovan. "As long as we're not paying, let's forget these too. By the way, that one's for you." He indicated the parcel.

Donovan picked it up. There was no return address. "Let's hope it's a care package." He tore off the brown wrapping and opened the box. The wallet was hidden among crumpled newspapers. He lifted it out slowly, turned it over. "I don't believe it. She sent it back."

Felix didn't bother to hide his astonishment. He looked over Donovan's shoulder as he opened the wallet and thumbed through the bills. "Complete with cash!" he crowed. "Hey, your lady is okay!"

Donovan had found the note sandwiched between a twenty and a fifty and was now reading it. She had kept it short and simple: "I'm sorry. Anna." That was all, but he felt as if he'd just touched her.

Suddenly he tossed the wallet aside and grabbed the discarded wrapping, turning it until he found the postmark. "Laguna Beach." He turned to Felix, his face alive with excitement. "Okay, this is your chance to prove out your big brags. Talk to some of these connections you claim to have and see if you can find out what's going on. I want to know what kind of trouble she's in and everybody who's looking for her."

"What good will that do? Look, Jay, I know you feel for this woman, but I'm telling you as a friend, don't get involved any more than you already are. Next time you might get more than a beating." Clearly agitated, Felix ran a hand through his heavy, dark hair.

"I'm already involved, more than I can explain. I need all the information you can come up with, then I'm going to Laguna Beach."

"Laguna Beach? Hell, you don't know that's where she is. She could have dropped it in a mailbox on her way through to anywhere."

Donovan shook his head, feeling more peaceful than he had in a long, long time. "No. She's there and I'm going."

Felix looked almost frantic. "This is crazy, Jay. How do you know you'll find her?"

"Because that's the way it's supposed to happen," Donovan said.

"I was afraid you'd say that." Felix sighed. "We've got to talk, *amigo*. There are a few things you need to know."

Donovan looked at his friend sharply, finally noticing the underlying note of tension in his voice and actions. He had a feeling he wasn't going to like what he heard.

The man impatiently tapped his *cigarillo* in the heavy marble ashtray. His dark brows drawn together in concentration, he pondered how things had deteriorated to this point. Had he truly been negligent, careless, or had fate contrived a series of events that no one, not even he, could have controlled?

This question had occupied much of his thinking in the past few days; it had seemed important to resolve his duplicity or lack of it, to develop an acceptable argument for El Patrón. Now he asked himself an even more important question: would it matter? No, he decided. El Patrón considered only results, not cause and effect, and results thus far had been pitifully inadequate.

For a while, it seemed as if he had a firm grip on the situation. Anna Michelotti was under surveillance and practically in his hands. Then the pressures had mounted. First he learned that Don Roberto's lawyers had ordered an audit of all the books, including the mining operations. A close investigation could uncover a supposedly dead mine that was unaccountably active. He must now go over the books before the audit, make certain there were no entries that couldn't be explained away.

Then he had received the catastrophic report from that *Norteamericano* bungler, saying the woman had disappeared, somehow slipping past his surveillance.

Something was wrong there. Anna had called, as he had expected her to, telling a story of unbearable grief that required time to bring under control. Nothing she had said indicated her intention to leave Southern California. Apparently she had felt safe enough to make contact, so why would she suddenly run away? Of course, he had not spoken to her himself, but he had no reason to doubt his source.

So what had happened? There were two possibilities. Either the detective had inadvertently alerted her to his presence, propelling her to flight, or else he was lying.

Unfortunately there was no time for sorting out the truth. Like *El Patrón*, one had to deal with results, not reasons. The only facts of any importance were that she possessed a dangerous knowledge and that she must be silenced in order to protect his own life.

Swiftly he reviewed the relevant data. She had not returned to her apartment in Los Angeles or to her job. And if that cretin had actually lost her trail, there were no more leads to follow.

Unless . . .

With sudden insight born of desperation, he picked up the phone, dialed a number, waited while the connection was made.

Then, "Listen carefully, Crewe. The woman has dropped out of sight. I believe that if she contacts anyone for help, it will be the pilot, Donovan. You're to follow him, watch him closely. He could lead us to her. No, no, bring her back here, to the mine. I told you that before, too. We aren't so well connected in the States that we can afford to call attention to ourselves. If you find her, wait until she's alone to take her. No, don't call here. I'll be in touch tomorrow."

When he replaced the receiver, his aristocratic features were grim. This could well be his last chance to redeem himself in El Patrón's eyes. He refused to think about the consequences if he failed to silence Anna Michelotti.

=6=

"I'LL LISTEN, BUT it won't change my mind." Donovan's irritation spilled over into short, nervous steps that took him from one side of the small room to the other. "And if it turns out you've been sitting on something that could've helped her, you better not stay long enough to tell me."

"Come on, Jay. You know I wouldn't do anything to hurt her, especially since . . . well, I can tell she's important to you."

"Damn right she is. So why are you trying to talk me out of going to California?"

Felix settled himself in the chair Donovan had just vacated. "Because we've been friends too long for me to just let it go. You've saved my butt more than once; maybe now I can return the favor."

"Hey, I appreciate friendly advice, but would you get to the point?"

"Yeah, sure." Felix shifted nervously. "I'm not even supposed to be talking about it, but . . . look, Jay, your lady may be involved in some very ugly activities, and if you're too close to her when the bust goes down, the implications could make things very uncomfortable for you."

" 'When the bust goes down'? Give me a break, Felix! You sound like Dirty Harry. Now, what the devil's going on?" Donovan's stride had lengthened as his anger mounted; now his feet planted themselves firmly beside Felix's chair.

"All right. About eighteen months ago, the flow of

illegals from the peninsula into the States took a sharp increase, and all the signs pointed to a tight, professional organization. Lots of front money, connections, bribes in high places."

"Michelotti." Donovan wasn't surprised. He'd heard lots of rumors about the old man and his criminal affiliations. "But I thought he'd gone legit."

Felix shrugged. "Maybe. Maybe not. That kind of life is a hard monkey to get off your back. Whatever, the whole Michelotti tribe is under suspicion."

"Including Anna." Donovan sat down on the corner of the desk, trying to fit the puzzle pieces together.

"Right. Her, the old man, Herrera, any one of half a dozen others who work out of Sonrisa. The island is the base for all the Michelotti businesses, and there are plenty of them. Imports, exports, mining, finance . . . big business makes for good cover."

"So where do you fit in?"

"An old buddy who works for the government now. We've kept in touch off and on, so when the investigation started down here, he asked me to pass along anything I thought he could use."

"And since I've been making regular runs to the island, you decided to let me do your spying for you." Donovan made a rude gesture. "Thanks a lot, buddy."

"*De nada.*" Felix grinned. "Don't worry, you make a lousy spy. I haven't been able to tell them anything so far."

Donovan wasn't amused. "So what am I supposed to do now? Back off? Throw her to the wolves?"

"What is this? You met her once and that makes you her protector?"

"Maybe it does. Whatever I feel, it's my problem."

Felix cleared his throat. "Jay, I . . . you know that running to her rescue won't make up for anything. I mean, if this is some kind of atonement for Fleur and your son . . .'"

"It has nothing to do with them." His tone made a flat statement: Subject closed.

Felix took the not-so-subtle hint. "Okay, *amigo*. I just wanted you to know what you're up against. If they pull your girlfriend in, you're likely to go right along with her. And going to the authorities for help won't get you very far. Most of the local police are playing footsie with Herrera. The Americans would just try to verify anything you said through channels, and since the lid's clamped on down here, they'd come up with exactly nothing and you'd look like a fool."

"Aw, don't encourage me too much, Felix, it might make me cocky." Donovan stood up, then leaned over the desk, bracing himself on his hands. "Since you're in the spy business now, how about plugging in for me on this one? See if you can find out what Herrera's up to, if he knows where Anna is now. If we're in a race for Laguna Beach, I'd rather have the inside track."

"I don't believe this." Felix sighed. "What happened to the Donovan Policy of Noninvolvement?"

"It died of boredom." It was Donovan's turn to grin. "Come on, get out your cloak and dagger, Ortiz. I'm going to need all the help I can get on this one."

Anna stirred and stretched, content for the moment to laze among the fluffy pillows and contemplate the day to come. From what she could see through the wide balcony doors, the morning was fine, bright and clear, probably quite cool, the sort of weather she thought perfect.

The past three days had been wonderfully peaceful and undisturbed. She'd done little but sleep, walk and occasionally sit by the pool in midafternoon when it was warmest, exchanging small talk with the two women who shared the condominium next to Wynette's. The serenity had worked a miracle with her emotional equilibrium. Though she still worried and grieved for her grandfather, the debilitating hopelessness had disappeared. It was a glorious feeling.

Rolling over with a yawn, she picked up the travel alarm she'd set out the night before and peered at it through tangled lashes. One o'clock! She couldn't remember the last time she'd slept so late, nearly eleven hours at one stretch. But, she reminded herself, it had been after two when she'd finally gone to bed.

She smiled, remembering how she'd walked on the beach the night before, for miles and miles, until her legs ached and she'd had to drop where she stood. As she rested, the mingled melody of the water and the ocean breeze had blown through her troubled thoughts and cleansed them, readying her for the healing process.

It had always been that way for her. One of her earliest memories was of wading through the surf on Sonrisa after her parents had died, drawing strength from the gentle beauty and serenity of the Sea of Cortez. Sand and water were her spiritual sustenance, natural tranquilizers that she could never get too much of.

Her new outlook was proof, if she'd ever needed it, of the value of her personal therapy. Sometime during the night, she'd put a period to the past and turned toward the future. She had stopped regretting and started anticipating.

Of course, she had to concede that her marathon walk didn't deserve all the credit for her altered state. Some of the pressure had been relieved with the telephone calls she'd made Tuesday.

She had talked first to Jim Collins, superintendent of the high school where she worked. He'd been solicitous, expressed his condolences, told her she was missed by faculty and students alike. When she asked him for another two weeks off, he had balked, relenting only when she reminded him of the sick leave she had accumulated over the past three years.

Umberto Salicido, her grandfather's legal advisor and oldest friend, had been next on her list. He politely inquired after her health, leaving her with the impression that he knew about—and disapproved of—her hasty departure from Sonrisa. Octavio, he told her, was a fine young man and would make her an excellent husband. Anna endured his well-meant meddling for several minutes, then got to the point of her call. He graciously answered her questions.

The probate would be finished in another ten days or so, he said, and she would be expected to return to Mexico to complete the legalities. *With pleasure*, she thought grimly.

The last call had been the most difficult, yet when it was over, she'd known a strange combination of relief and reassurance. 'Tavio had sounded the same as always—forthright, affectionate, caring . . .

"Anna!" he had exclaimed, his voice rich with delighted surprise. "*Querida*, are you all right? I've been sick with worry."

For a moment, she had felt like nothing had happened—those horrible, incriminating words had never been spoken, she had never learned what 'Tavio really was. If she had allowed herself to, she could so easily have fallen into the warmth and normalcy she had imagined was there and promised to return to the island, to 'Tavio and the security her grandfather had planned for her.

But she had looked at her surroundings, remembering how she had come to be there, and the illusion had faded.

So she had told the story she had rehearsed, letting all the genuine grief and bewilderment she felt come to the forefront.

"I know, 'Tavio, and I'm so sorry for leaving the way I did, without saying anything. It was just so painful, the funeral and all the memories. I thought I'd lose my mind if I stayed another moment, so I just . . . ran."

"With Donovan?" He sounded neither skeptical nor accepting, merely curious.

Hearing him speak Donovan's name caught her off-guard. "Donovan? Oh, the pilot. Yes, he was leaving, so I talked him into taking me along. Then I called a friend to arrange a flight back to L.A."

"But *querida*, you left everything here—your clothes and money. Are you sure you're telling me everything?"

She had expected the questions, planned for them. But lying didn't come easily for her; the thought of making a mistake, tripping herself up, left her mouth dry. "Of course

I am. Oh, 'Tavio, please don't worry, and don't be angry. It was foolish and impulsive, but I'm all right now."

"So you're in Los Angeles. Where are you staying? I've phoned you at home every day."

"With friends," she said quickly. "I still don't like being alone at night. Look, I promise I'll be back in a couple of weeks, and we can go ahead with the plans for the wedding. If you still want to, of course."

He had laughed. "If I want to? What a strange and lovely girl you are. I miss you, *querida*. Just take care of yourself and hurry back to me."

"I miss you too." The words had nearly choked her. "Don't worry about me, all right? I'll be in touch soon."

'Tavio was silent for a moment. Then, "Anna, I wish you'd come back. Or at least tell me where you are."

"Please. I really need this time to myself, 'Tavio. I still haven't quite . . . adjusted."

"All right, *querida*. I understand."

She had sighed with relief. "Thank you, 'Tavio. Goodbye . . ."

She sat up in bed and stretched again. Enough of that, she thought. There was no way of knowing if she'd convinced him; only time would prove it one way or the other. Meanwhile, there was a great slice of autumn waiting for her, and Wynette would arrive soon for the weekend. She would focus her attention on enjoying the weather and the company.

Rolling out of bed, she padded into the bathroom, slipped out of her gown and stepped into the shower. Several minutes later, she smiled when she realized the melody bouncing around the tiles was coming from her. She was singing.

"I just don't know if I'm cut out for this," Wynette said, flipping idly through the pages of a fashion magazine she'd picked up earlier at the supermarket.

Anna didn't look up from her manicure-in-progress. "Cut out for what?"

"All this junk." Long brown fingers swept across a two-page spread adorned with several elegantly clad women, one of whom was Wynette, clustered around one lone male in white tie and tails. The bold lettering across the bottom of the pages proclaimed that the cologne in question would "make every man's fantasy come true." "I mean, look at me, draped all over that guy, tryin' to look 'wild with desire.' No foolin', girl, that's what the photographer said. 'Now, ladies,' " she mimicked in an affected drawl, " 'this man is your ideal, and he's driving you wild with desire. Let's have a little healthy panting.' " She hooted with laughter, along with Anna, whose attention had been successfully diverted from the red enamel on her nails.

"Let me see that," Anna said.

Wynette obligingly held up the magazine while Anna peered at it.

Anna made a moue of approval. "He's gorgeous, Wyn. I might be persuaded to do a little panting of my own."

"Not likely," Wynette snorted. "We started shooting this layout at six in the mornin', worked 'til two that afternoon, then I went straight across town to another one that didn't wrap 'til after midnight. Not one of my better days. I haven't had enough energy to pant after anything."

"Sounds like a bad case of disillusionment. But you knew it would be rough when you started, and think of how far you've come, Wyn. There are a million girls who'd love to trade places with you."

"Well, I'm thinkin' about takin' applications. Wanna help?"

"Hey, you're not serious, are you? What happened to the dream?"

Wynette sighed. "Oh, it's still there. Don't pay any attention to me, I'm just tired. I'm gonna stick with it another two years, and by then I'll have enough saved to go on to college and not have to worry about workin'. Oh, look at this, girl! That's got to be the most beautiful gown. It'd look great on you. Have you picked out your wedding dress yet?"

"No, not yet. There's plenty of time." Studiously, Anna bent to her nails again.

After a few seconds' silence, she raised her head to find Wynette staring at her. "What?" she said sharply.

Wynette shrugged. "Nothin', I guess. But you sure don't act like any bride-to-be I ever knew. Even when you first told me about it last year, you weren't—I don't know, bubbly, excited. And when I mentioned it just now, you sorta went away."

"It's just not that kind of arrangement, Wyn. It's hard to explain."

"Arrangement?" Wynette's widened eyes reflected her astonishment. "Now, you gotta explain that one, girl."

Anna hoped her friend couldn't see that the small brush she held was far from steady. "It's not medieval, Wynette. But I've always known I'd probably marry 'Tavio. I know him better than anyone else, we share all the same things, and it's what Poppy wanted."

"What about what you want?"

"If I hadn't wanted it, I'd have said so. Look, you're making a big deal over nothing."

"So if it's nothin', why do it? I mean, marriage is supposed to be forever, and if this 'Tavio is good enough for forever, he should be good enough to put stars in your eyes."

"It's not like that!" Anna said angrily. "I haven't had stars in my eyes since college, and I let them blind me twice. The first guy turned out to have a wife and kids; I thought he worked nights. The second one was even better." She shook her head. This was the first time she'd thought of him in years, and she still couldn't believe she'd been so ignorant. "I took him to Sonrisa, introduced him to Poppy and my friends. I was really in love. But Poppy knew, he tried to tell me, but I wouldn't listen. So Poppy handled it himself. He offered Gary fifty thousand dollars to get lost, and Gary accepted. Poppy taped the conversation and played it back for me later." She laughed mirthlessly. "Of course, Gary didn't get his money. Anyway, I figured I was such a lousy judge of character, why not do what my grandfather wanted? 'Tavio was like a part of the family, and he was really my best friend, next to Poppy."

"Was?"

The single word clearly pointed up Anna's mistake and she was silent.

"Sounds like you're talkin' past tense, girl," Wynette pressed. "So what's happened? Either he's turned out to be a dud too, or you met somebody else. Which is it?"

"Oh, I do wish you'd hush." Donovan popped into her head again. Even if all the ugliness hadn't happened, how could she marry 'Tavio when she knew she would never respond to him the way she had to Donovan? And a tiny voice inside echoed, *You'll never respond to anyone else that way, and you know it.* But she still wasn't ready to talk about it, not even to Wynette. "You make me sound like a character in a soap opera. Speaking of which, weren't you up for a part in something? How did that turn out?"

Wynette cocked her head to one side as if to say, "Okay, you win this one, but it's not finished." Aloud she said, "Same ole thing. I read for it and they said, 'Don't call us—' "

" '—we'll call you.' "

Feeling on safer ground now, Anna managed to swing the conversation into more normal channels. She finished her nails to the rhythm of Wynette's patter, learning more than she really wanted to know about the world of modeling.

Hours later, Wynette poured them both a glass of wine and turned on the small television set she'd brought from her apartment in L.A. "May as well see what's goin' on in the wide world. Somebody may have declared war."

A news program was on and Anna watched contentedly,

not really paying attention to what the announcer was saying. Then the editorial segment aired.

"Unfortunately, the latest tragedy is not an isolated incident," the announcer was saying. "The eighteen bodies found in the Sonoran desert represent only a small percentage of the lives that have been lost in recent years. Every advancement in law enforcement and detection is seemingly countered by more elaborate methods of transportation . . ."

In horror, she listened to the voice drone on, watched the pictures that flashed across the screen. *Murder*, she thought, *it was murder. And 'Tavio was a part of it.*

Her stomach churned. God, was she doing the right thing by waiting? What if it happened again before she went to the authorities? Wouldn't she then be as guilty as 'Tavio and the men who worked for him?

And, by association, her thoughts turned to Donovan and she began to doubt again. He could be involved too. Maybe her initial suspicions were right after all, and she had simply rationalized them away, talked herself into believing a lie because it was easier that way.

"Hey, what's wrong? You look sick."

Wynette was there beside her, taking the wine glass from her hand. "Anna, answer me! Are you all right?"

"No," she managed, "I don't feel well. I think I'd better go to bed." She stood up shakily. "Don't worry, I think it's just an upset stomach. I ate a lot more than usual tonight."

"I told you that stuff was too spicy," Wynette said, touching her face. "You don't have a fever. Look, you get in bed and I'll bring you somethin' to settle your stomach."

Anna lay awake a long time, and when she finally slept, her dreams were filled with faceless terrors that pursued her through the desert.

"I really wish you wouldn't do this, Jay." Felix maneuvered the car to the unloading area of the airport terminal. "What if she doesn't want to come back with you?"

"I'll think of something," Donovan answered. "I'll call when I get there, let you know where I'm staying." He hefted his travel bag out of the backseat and opened the car door. "You just keep snooping around in case Herrera decides to make a sudden trip. And stop worrying."

"Sure," Felix said with a lopsided smile. "And listen, if you run into any trouble, you know I'll be there. Just give a yell."

While he waited for his flight to be called, Donovan shook a cigarette from the new pack of Camels and lit it. He really hadn't given much thought to what he would do if she refused to come back with him, but he didn't let it concern him too much. If necessary, he'd stuff her in a duffel bag and carry her back over his shoulder.

The thing that did concern him was Herrera. From all outward appearances, the man was going about his business as usual. He'd planned no trips, cancelled no appointments, and that in itself worried Donovan. He didn't trust anything that was too easy.

But there was nothing he could do about it now. He'd just take things as they came. The first order of business was finding Anna, then persuading her to trust him. *Take a chance on me, sweetheart*, he willed. *I won't let you down.*

= 7 =

THE NEXT TWO DAYS were better, and Anna began to regain some of the precious balance she needed so badly.

On Saturday she and Wynette went shopping. Actually, to Anna it was more of a binge. Following Wynette around the mall, she was reminded of those contest winners who had five minutes to put as much as possible into the cart. By the time they got back to the apartment, Wynette's small car bulged with packages and boxes that contained everything from glassware to groceries.

As soon as they unloaded that haul, Wynette was pushing her out the door again.

"Wyn, I'm too tired for any more of this," Anna protested. "If I walk anymore, my feet will fall off."

"Uh-uh, girl, you're not gettin' off that easy. We're gonna get you some clothes. I'm about sick of seein' those jeans." She looked Anna's thin form up and down. "For somebody with class, that is absolutely pitiful."

In the face of such solid reasoning, Anna felt she could do nothing but relent gracefully, and off they went again.

Slacks, blouses, sweaters—even hats, which Anna never wore—fell by the wayside, victims of Wynette's relentless quest for perfection.

"Trash," she declared a dozen times, "this stuff is pure trash. We gotta find somethin' that says, 'Hey, world, this is Anna Michelotti!'"

"If it's all the same to you, I prefer a whisper to a shout," Anna retorted, discarding a pair of magenta ankle pants with diagonal slashes of green. "Can't we look at something just a trifle less conspicuous?"

"Party pooper. I bet you'd rather browse through the exclusive Levi section?"

"Great idea!" Anna teased. "I'm so glad you thought of it."

On the way out of the juniors department, Wynette giggled. "Hope he's buyin' that for somebody besides himself," she said, indicating a man who stood by a rack of sweaters.

He was of medium height and slightly balding, with a serious, somehow sad expression that was at odds with the wild orange baggy sweater he was holding up for inspection.

Anna smiled at the idea of the man mincing in front of a floor-length mirror, turning this way and that to check the fit of the fuzzy sweater. Then he turned slightly, lifted his gaze, and their eyes met.

Unreasonably, Anna felt uncomfortable. Not that there was anything offensive about his look; they were merely two strangers exchanging glances, yet she could almost imagine some deeper contact had been made.

Then Wynette drew her attention to a mannequin bedecked in head-to-toe leather, and Anna shrugged off the notion as fanciful nonsense.

They shopped until the stores closed and once again lugged a multitude of packages through the brightly lit parking lot to the car.

"This is ridiculous. We spend *hours* going through every store in town, to get *me* some clothes, she says," Anna grumbled. "I am now the proud owner of one jumpsuit and two sore feet, and *you* wind up with enough to fill a warehouse."

Wynette unlocked the doors and they began tossing the parcels inside. "You're just outta practice. Stick around a while and I'll get you whipped back into shape."

"Whipped is right. At least I shouldn't have any trouble sleeping tonight."

True to her prediction, Anna wasted no time getting into bed. Once she woke from a dream, frightened, but she couldn't remember what she'd been running from, only that there was a haven waiting for her at the end of her journey. *Prophecy or wishful thinking?* she wondered sleepily, and drifted off again.

The detective stopped on the street, watching the two women safely into their parking area. He'd have preferred to leave his car and get closer, make sure they were inside before he left. But the Michelotti girl had seen him tonight in the store, and he didn't want to chance her spotting him again. There was no point in frightening her.

He wasn't sure how much longer he'd stick around; he should have been gone already. It wasn't his problem anymore. He'd already stuck his neck out for her, lying to the man in Mexico. But every time he tried to walk away he thought of Jeannie. If he left now, without knowing this woman was all right, it would be like running out on Jeannie. When he went back to her, he wanted to do it proudly, like the man he used to be.

He watched them unload the car and disappear around the corner of the building, then he left his vehicle and followed. A light came on in their apartment, so he walked through the complex, then back again. He'd seen no one there, had made sure they weren't followed from the mall.

He decided to go on home and get some sleep, start again tomorrow. He'd done all he could to protect her tonight.

Three days.

Three days of waiting, watching, walking the beach for hours until his knee nearly buckled with pain and his body ached with fatigue.

Three days of searching the streets of Laguna Beach for a skinny blonde, of following strange women to restaurants and through stores because the backs of their heads looked like Anna's.

Three days of falling into the uncomfortable motel room

at four o'clock in the morning, then waking a few hours later to start all over again. The only good news he'd had was the last phone call to Felix: his mysterious government friend had agreed to offer Anna protection as a material witness, providing she came straight to him and didn't compromise the investigation by going to the police. Other than that bit of news, his time in California was memorable only for its lack of sleep and progress.

Now here he was, facing another midnight vigil.

The strain was increasing with each nonproductive day, his optimism beginning to slip away. The task in itself was monumental. How could he ever have hoped to find one person, especially one who didn't want to be found, among the population of a place like Laguna Beach? And the race against time compounded the problem.

Herrera had all the resources: he could hire private detectives, contact Anna's friends, probably even check her bank account for recent withdrawals. Donovan's only aces were a strong instinct for survival and the impetus of this strange emotional whirlpool that had drawn him to this place at this time.

So with nothing else to rely on, he opted to trust his instinct, and it told him that if she went no other place in this town, she would come here, to the ocean. If he waited long enough, he knew, she would come. She had to—her life depended on it.

An hour passed, and another. The wind blowing off the water was cold, and he pulled his field jacket tighter around his neck. Across the water he could see the whiteness of a fog bank rolling in, slowly edging its way toward land. He smiled. Was this his destiny, to eternally wait for Anna to appear from the mist?

He walked to the edge of the water and gazed at the moonlit breakers. For perhaps fifteen minutes he stood there, thinking about another night very like this one, wondering if he should bless or curse the changes it had brought to his life.

Then he stiffened, aware of a subtle altering of the night's stillness. Something was going to happen, he could feel it in the air, in the way his senses had suddenly heightened.

He felt her presence before he saw her. The magic worked on him like a radio receiver, attuning him to her movements. When he turned, she was only a few yards away, walking toward him as though she'd known he would be there.

She stopped very near to him and tilted her face up to look into his eyes. "I dreamed about you last night," she said softly, "that you would be here like this."

"I dream about you every night," he responded, staring at her in wonder.

"What's happening to me, to us? I can't understand it—" Her voice broke, just a little, and she turned her face away.

"Anna, some things aren't meant to be understood."

She came into his arms then and he held her for a long time, savoring the feel and smell of her.

"How did you find me?" she asked finally.

"I read the postmark."

"Oh. I didn't think of that." She looked at him quizzically. "How long have you been here?"

"Three days."

"That's a long time to stand on the beach."

"I'd have stayed as long as it took." Touching her face gently with only two fingers, he turned it up to meet the moonlight. "But I'm glad I didn't have to wait any longer."

He kissed her and she let him, not quite responding, though he sensed she wanted to.

"Why are you here?" she asked when he released her lips.

"To take you back with me. Did you feel it?" He thought she must surely hear his heart pounding.

"Feel what?"

"The magic." He touched her hair, her face.

"I don't know what I feel." She pulled away from his hand. "What do you mean, take me back? To Mexico?"

"To Guaymas, until all this is over. You'll be safer there." He wanted to take her in his arms again but knew she wouldn't allow it.

"You know then." Her tone held an accusation.

"Some. I know your boyfriend's suspected of trading in wetbacks, and I know you're hiding from him, probably because you know something you shouldn't." He watched her reaction.

"Suspected?" Her eyes widened. "You mean the authorities know?"

He couldn't be certain, but he thought she sounded relieved. " 'Under investigation' is the way I heard it."

"Heard it from whom?" The accusation was back.

"Why don't you say it, Anna, straight out so there's no chance I'll misunderstand."

She thrust her chin out in what he felt sure was an unconscious gesture of bravado, and for the first time he let his mind form the word his heart had been feeling all along: love.

"Do you work for 'Tavio?" she asked.

Though the question was broad, he understood the specific meaning; in fact, he'd been expecting it.

"Anna," he said levelly, meeting her eyes, "I'm part owner of a helicopter charter service. I fly people where they want to go and they pay me for it. But I don't work for any of them, not in the way you mean. I've never even met Herrera."

"Then how do you know about all this, about me?"

"Because a man named Crewe came to see me. Somebody figured out that you'd left the island with me. Crewe wanted to know where you were."

"Crewe? I don't know anyone by that name."

She looked lost, he thought, like a child wandering through the maze of mirrors at a carnival. She also looked cold, in spite of the bulky turtleneck sweater she wore, for she shivered and hugged herself.

He pulled her to him again and held her tightly. "Oh, Anna, we can't come up with all the answers right now. There are too many questions. Just trust me, come back with me. I'm not sure how you fit into all this, but you probably found out too much about Herrera's business, right?"

She nodded.

"Then you're a material witness. The American feds have guaranteed protection for you."

She accepted his embrace, laid her cheek against his chest. But he could tell that her seeming acquiescence was merely a cover for her next argument.

"You're throwing around a lot of information, Donovan, and that bothers me. You know too much for a helicopter pilot who just flies people where they want to go."

He held her away from his body just enough to see her face. He tried to put all the conviction he could muster into his voice, terribly aware of how crucial his words would be.

"Anna, listen to me. I wouldn't be here now if I didn't care for you. Finding you, keeping you safe, is the most important thing in my life. I'm lucky enough to have a friend who knows what's going on and is willing to help me. Whatever I know, I only found out after the fact. I am not involved with smuggling illegal aliens. I do not work for Herrera. And I would never do anything to harm you."

She answered in a whisper and he had to strain to hear. "I'm scared, Jay." It was the first time she'd ever used his given name. *Closer*, he thought, *we're getting closer*. "Nothing's the way it used to be, the way it should be . . . why can't we just stay here?"

He didn't miss that *we*. Somewhere along the way she'd accepted that they were a unit, neither of them complete without the other.

"Because we'd be too vulnerable. Herrera has all the heavy ammo, honey. All I've got is a slingshot."

This time it was she who initiated the embrace as she

burrowed deeply into his jacket front. He marveled at the sense of unity and peace that enveloped them both.

"I'll go back with you," she said softly. "It may be the worst mistake I've ever made, but I trust you." Her arms slid around him. "But there's one condition."

"What?"

"That we don't have to stay at the Victory Bar."

He squeezed her, elated, then they turned and began walking. Everything would work out now. "We can leave tonight, right now. I have a rented car—"

"No," she interrupted. "I'm staying with a friend, and I have to tell her I'm leaving. Besides, there are a few things I need to work out, and I don't think so clearly when I'm with you." She smiled at him. "I'll meet you in the morning, after she's gone to work."

Her suggestion left him feeling edgy, but he'd pushed her far enough. "Okay," he agreed, "the night's almost over anyway. Where does your friend live?"

She gestured back over her shoulder. "There are some condominiums about half a mile up the beach. I'll be waiting in the parking lot."

"I'll walk you back."

She shook her head. "I'll be okay. Don't try to box me in, Donovan." Her fingers traced his jaw, then she walked away.

Donovan stood watching long after the darkness had swallowed her up, praying he'd done the right thing in letting her go one last time.

Crewe followed Anna at a discreet distance. Because of the darkness and the fog, he nearly lost her a couple of times, finally drew closer than he'd intended and watched her go into a door marked 117. As soon as the door closed behind her, the outside light went off.

From the shadows he surveyed the complex. There were four buildings, two on each side of the pool area, which was fenced and backed by a cabana. The covered parking area ran behind the buildings parallel to the street, accessed by sidewalks running between.

Number 117 was the lower apartment, inside corner of the southernmost building.

Skirting the bright patches cast by the wall-mounted security lights, Crewe made his way to the corner of that building until he stood near the door she'd entered. He edged past it to the long front window and positioned himself to look through the narrow slit left by the incomplete closing of the drapes.

The room was lit. He could see his quarry seated near the back wall, and seconds later another person crossed his vision, brushing the draperies so that they parted, letting the light fall across his startled face. He darted to the side, back into the shadows.

Not tonight, then. The boss said to take her quietly, attract no attention.

He would have to wait, but not for long.

"Sure you gonna be okay?" Wynette had asked the same question several times that morning, clearly nervous about Anna's abrupt decision to leave.

"Of course I'm sure," Anna answered patiently. "Hey, I thought we talked this out last night. Wynette, I know what I'm doing." *I hope*, she added to herself. But she wouldn't burden Wynette with her indecision. "Now, you go on to work before you're late. I'll lock up everything here and turn your rental car in at the airport, so don't worry about that. And I'll call you tonight, let you know I'm all right."

Wynette was unwilling to be mollified. "You haven't been all right since you got here, so I don't expect things will change by tonight," she grumbled, picking up her jacket off the arm of the sofa. "I should be home by eight, and I'm gonna be waitin' for that call."

Anna knew how upset her friend was. When she'd come in the night before, Wynette had been awake, walking the floor. When she'd announced her decision to leave, Wynette had reacted with uncharacteristic anger, sparking an argument that apparently hadn't been forgotten.

"Look, Wyn, I appreciate all you've done, but I shouldn't have to tell you that. And I know you've been worried about me. I wish I could tell you what's going on, but I still think I'm right. If you don't know anything, then you can't be involved, and that's the way it's got to be."

"Not involved?" Wynette threw up her hands in exasperation. "You're my *friend*, Anna! Remember that word, *friendship?* I love you, I'm worried—no, not worried. I'm *scared* for you." She paced around the sofa. "First you're breakin' your neck to get out of Mexico and back here, to—to hide out. That's what it was, and I know it! I sneak you out here, tuck you away outta sight of whatever you're runnin' from, and now you're on your way back, no explanations, no nothin', and you wanna keep me *uninvolved?*"

"But, Wyn . . ."

Her black eyes snapping with anger, Wyn kicked the unfortunate floor pillow next to her foot. "Do you know that you cry in your sleep? Sometimes you moan and talk, fast and all jumbled up. I've watched you starin' out the window for hours, girl, *hours*, not talkin', not movin'. Last night I woke up and you were gone, and I nearly *died*, thinkin' you'd been kidnapped or killed! Now how much more *involved* do I have to get before you start givin' me some straight answers?"

Shocked, Anna could only stare at her friend. She'd had no inkling that Wynette had been harboring so much frustration and resentment.

"Oh, Wyn, I'm so sorry. I shouldn't have come here in the first place; it was unfair to you. I'll explain it all someday, but for now I have to do—"

"I know, I know. You have to do what you think best. Lord, am I sick of hearin' that!" She snatched her purse off the end table and headed for the front door. "Just forget it, okay? I gotta go to work."

Then she was gone, leaving the door standing open.

Anna wanted to run after her, call her to come back, but she didn't. There would be time for explanation when it was over. Their friendship was strong, and Wynette would understand when she knew the whole story.

Pushing herself to action, Anna ran upstairs, slipped out of her gown and robe and into jeans and a long-sleeved, plaid shirt. She'd told Donovan to meet her at nine, and it was already nearly eight-thirty. Thank goodness she'd done her packing the night before.

When she finished dressing, she stood in front of the mirrored dresser to brush her hair, pulling it back into a large clip low on her neck.

A noise on the stairs drew her attention. "Wyn, did you forget something?" There was no answer. "Wyn?"

A frisson of fear rippled across her skin, a breath of apprehension, and she shivered. *The door. I didn't close the front door.*

She laid the brush on the dresser top and noticed as she did so that her hand trembled. Another sound, so faint she could almost believe she had imagined it, froze her muscles. She stood still, moving first her eyes, to the mirror and up. Then she raised her head.

He stood in the doorway behind her, his heavy features arranged in a facsimile of a smile. His gray suit looked crumpled, as if he'd slept in it, and his jowls were stubbled with a stiff growth of whiskers.

Their eyes met in the mirror.

She watched him open his mouth to speak, and her throat constricted.

"Howya doin'?"

She swallowed. "What do you want?"

His mirrored eye winked at her. "You got everybody all upset, runnin' away like that. They sent me to make sure you got home okay."

She felt like she was suffocating, like the air was being sucked out of the space where she stood. His eyes were hateful, gloating, yet she couldn't look away from the mirror.

She watched as he took a step forward into the room.

She swallowed again, trying to fight down the rising panic. "How did you find me?"

His smile broadened. "Piece of cake, thanks to your friend Donovan."

Her breathlessness slid into nausea. *No, no, no. He wouldn't do this to me, not Donovan. He said I could trust him. He promised* . . .

Incomprehension and a numbed disbelief held her rigid. He took another step toward her, then another, but still she couldn't move. Inconsequentially she noticed that in spite of his bulk he made no noise when he walked, like a cat creeping up on its prey.

Another noise from downstairs, then Wynette's voice shattered the silence and broke the spell.

"Anna? Hey, girl, I'm sorry I left like that . . ." Her heels clicked across the hardwood floor, then up the stairs.

Anna snatched up the hairbrush, whirled and threw it at the man's head with startling accuracy, shouting, "Run, Wyn, get out of here!"

The man recoiled when the brush bounced off his forehead, then he surged forward. Anna met his attack, clawing and scratching, twisting away from his cruel grip, fighting to get out of the room.

Suddenly Wynette was there, flying around the room, yelling. "What's goin' on? Who is this jerk? Get your hands off her, creep!"

With a deft, quick move he spun behind Anna, and she found her back pressed against his hard chest and stomach, his left arm encircling her midriff. She opened her mouth to scream, then thought better of it when she saw the ugly, snub-nosed pistol he held in his right hand.

He waved the gun twice to make his point. "You, legs, you shut up. Just move over to the corner behind the bed and stay put."

"Fat chance, turkey. I'm not goin' nowhere 'til you let her go." The bravado didn't quite cover up the quaver in Wynette's voice.

The man laughed. "Gutsy broad, but not too smart. You ever been shot?"

Anna's heart threatened to burst from her chest. "For God's sake, Wyn, don't argue with him!"

"Listen to your friend, honey, and get outta the way." He prodded Anna forward with his knee. Her feet didn't want to comply and it took another harder nudge to get her moving.

Wynette stood braced in the doorway, not giving an inch. "You're not leavin' with her . . ."

"My God, Wyn, *please* . . ." Images of Wynette, still and bloodied, left Anna limp with terror.

"Last chance, babe," he growled, waving the pistol again and pushing his hostage to take another stumbling step.

Anna looked at the younger woman's stubbornly set face, no longer cafe au lait but ash gray, and knew she had to act.

She jerked her head back sharply with a force that snapped her neck, connecting with the man's face. He grunted with pain and surprise and reeled back. Seizing the gun with both hands, she threw her weight on his arm. At the edge of her vision, Wyn darted toward the bed.

The man cursed, flung Anna against the dresser and raised the pistol. Blood streamed from his nose, painting his contorted features with garish rage. The gun barrel didn't waver as it seemed to inch upward. To Anna, it appeared to grow bigger, darker, more evil, until it loomed like a deadly tunnel, sucking her in . . .

Then Wynette was there behind him, throwing a bedspread over his head, wrapping her long limbs around his shrouded body.

"Get outta here!" she screamed at Anna, riding the bucking, twisting form.

Instead of obeying Wynette's frantic command, Anna dove for the man's knees and he went down, screaming obscenities. His wrist cracked against the dresser and the gun went flying. She leapt onto the heap with Wynette, both of them struggling to hold him down.

Wynette stretched her long frame toward the dresser, grabbed the heavy ceramic lamp, yanking the cord out of the wall. Anna watched dumbfounded as her friend brought the weighted base down hard on the man's covered head. He yelped, then lay still.

The women rose from his prostrate form, looked at each other.

"Now what?" Anna gasped.

"Now you get your tail outta here," Wyn ordered, scooping up the fallen gun and Anna's suitcase. "Any idea where you're goin'?" She pushed Anna toward the stairs.

"Not yet," Anna replied shakily. "I'll let you know when I get there."

"Take my car, the keys are in it. Give me the ones to the rental. Got enough money?"

"Yes. Wyn, I . . ."

"I know, girl. I love you too."

Anna's purse, one she'd bought under protest only a few days before, hung by its strap from the newel post. She grabbed it and quickly fished out the keys and handed them to Wyn, who hustled her out the front door, giving her a quick hug and the suitcase. "Now will you please go away?"

"Wynette, he's dangerous . . ."

"Yeah, but I'm out here now." She shoved gently. "Go on."

Anna dashed between the buildings to the parking lot.

Behind her, she could hear Wynette yelling, "Help! Somebody help me!"

On the highway, the tires hummed with an all-too-familiar refrain.

Run, Anna, run . . .

=8=

DONOVAN PULLED INTO the parking lot and stopped, then looked at his watch nervously. No need for her to be here yet—he was twenty minutes early. He put the car into gear again and moved into an empty space about halfway down the row that faced the backs of the buildings.

Directly in front of him, a sidewalk ran between the buildings. For perhaps a minute he sat, until through the gap he noticed several people running, all in the same direction. An unease crept into the automobile with him and, in a matter of seconds, grew into gnawing anxiety.

He leapt from the car, slamming the door into a support post, and dashed between the buildings, coming out near a swimming pool. Across the concrete expanse, a small crowd was gathered in front of a corner apartment.

His heart thumping furiously, Donovan approached. A young black woman sat on the lone step leading to the front door, holding a cloth to her temple. When she removed the cloth for a moment, he could see an ugly swelling that was already turning bluish.

"What happened?" he asked an elderly woman standing next to him.

"Why, I'm not sure," she answered. "I heard someone screaming and ran outside to see, and there was that young woman, yelling her head off." She indicated Wynette, who was looking more unwell by the second. "She was holding a gun and shouting for help. Then this man came running out her door, knocked her down and poof! he was gone."

She shook her head. "Poor thing, I thought she was dead for a minute, just laying there like that. Hit her head, you know."

"Who is she?"

"Wynette something, Fitzpatrick, I think. She's new here, a model, someone told me."

He scanned all the faces anxiously, but even as he looked he knew he wouldn't see Anna. He'd blown it by letting her come back here last night.

The crowd parted as he shouldered his way through to kneel beside the injured woman.

"Where's Anna?" he asked.

Startled, she drew back from him. "Who are you?"

"Donovan. She was supposed to meet me this morning; now where is she?" He heard his voice rising and cut off the words. "I'm sorry, but you've got to talk to me."

The woman was obviously nervous, but she met Donovan's eyes squarely. "How do I know you didn't have somethin' to do with what happened?"

He gritted his teeth. He wanted to shake her, force her to understand. Instead he said evenly, "You'll have to take my word for it. Just tell me if she's okay."

Wynette studied him for a moment, then apparently made up her mind.

"Yeah, she got out. Took my car and left."

The knot in Donovan's gut loosened. "Where did she go?"

"We didn't have time to plan an itinerary." She touched her bruised temple gingerly and winced. "She wasn't thinkin' about much of anything except gettin' outta here. But she did say she'd call later."

"So tell me what happened."

She sighed. "Lord, I don't know for sure. I'd left already, then I came back and here was this guy with a gun tryin' to drag her off."

"Got any idea who he was?"

A male voice intruded into their conversation. "I do."

Donovan and Wynette both turned their heads sharply to look at the newcomer. A nondescript man in early middle age, he wore the tired, defeated look of a heavy drinker. His slacks and lightweight sports coat weren't exactly shabby, but he obviously hadn't budgeted for new clothes in a good while. In one hand he carried a snub-nosed gun, which he offered to Wynette.

"You dropped this when you fell," he said.

Donovan intercepted the weapon, turned it over in his hands. "You have a name?" he asked the stranger.

"Barnes. Frank Barnes. I'm a private detective."

His eyes met Donovan's and held, a message lurking somewhere behind the pale blue irises. Donovan thought it looked strangely like regret.

"You know something about this," Donovan stated, feeling his hackles rise.

Barnes nodded. "More than I want to." He gestured toward the thinning crowd. "Maybe we could talk inside."

"Best idea I've heard all day," said Wynette, who'd watched the byplay between the two men in confusion. "I don't have enough padding for this concrete."

She tried to stand, but her wobbly legs didn't cooperate. Donovan slipped his arm around her waist to steady her. She was surprisingly tall, over six feet, and elegantly thin.

Just then the woman he'd spoken to earlier hurried over, her pleasantly lined face avid with curiosity.

"How are you, dear?" she cooed. "I'd be glad to help you inside. You should get right into bed and rest."

"Thanks, but I'm okay. It's just a bump." Wynette turned away, allowing Donovan to guide her to the front door, which still gaped open.

"All right, dear, if you're sure. I'm Mrs. Harris, and if you need anything, just sing out. And don't you worry. Mr. Brancuzzi called the police. They'll have that dreadful man behind bars in no time."

For a moment it appeared as if Mrs. Harris would follow them into the apartment, but she stopped just short of having the door shut in her face.

Inside, Donovan held Wynette's elbow until she was seated on the plump-cushioned sofa. Frank Barnes stood alone in the center of the room, looking more defeated than ever.

Donovan turned to face him. "Okay, Barnes, you say you know the guy?"

"Yeah. I used to see him around in San Diego about five years ago. We . . . worked in the same circles."

"So what's his name?"

"Crewe—that's all I ever heard."

Somehow Donovan had expected to hear the name. Herrera had been closer than he thought. Damn! Why had he let her go last night? He could have *made* her stay with him if he'd tried, and now they'd have been on their way to the airport together. But like a jerk, he hadn't wanted to pressure her. Because of his stupidity, she'd nearly been kidnapped, probably with murder in mind, and he didn't have the first clue where to start looking for her.

"I remember you now," Wynette said, breaking the uncomfortable silence. She was looking at Barnes. "You were in the department store on Saturday. Yeah, and I saw you here yesterday, outside."

Barnes offered no comment beyond looking guilty.

"You've been tailing Anna?" When Barnes nodded, Donovan's fists clenched convulsively. "You've got two seconds to start spilling your guts, Barnes, or I'm going to take you apart."

Wynette shrank into the cushions, frightened beyond words by the venom in Donovan's voice. She had absolutely no doubt that he'd do exactly what he threatened, and do it with relish.

Barnes's lips twisted in a parody of mirth. "That's why I'm here, friend," he said, with the first flicker of emotion he'd shown, "to spill my guts."

"Who hired you and why?" Donovan demanded, although he was already certain of the answer.

"I don't know why," Barnes answered. "About a week ago I got a call from Mexico, a man I owed. He told me to watch the airport for her, follow her and report back. He telefaxed her picture to a company he owns in L.A."

"You weren't supposed to pick her up?" Donovan hadn't relaxed a whit; his stance was rigid, aggressive.

"No, just follow her and report, like I said."

"You did a good job, buddy. Crewe nearly had her."

"Not because of me," Barnes denied quietly. "I reported when she got to L.A. and then when she went to Miss Fitzpatrick's apartment. But not when she moved in here. I told him I lost her."

"Why?"

"That's my business. Maybe I just don't have the stomach for this kind of thing anymore."

"Then why are you still hangin' around?" Wynette chimed in. "She's been here since Tuesday."

Barnes shrugged. "I asked myself the same question. I just wanted to . . . watch out for her."

"You weren't watching too damned well, were you?" Donovan snapped. "Crewe's hard to miss."

Barnes turned his sad countenance on Donovan. "I'm afraid you'll have to take the credit for that. Crewe didn't show up until you did. I think you led him here yourself."

During the deafening silence that followed, Donovan was aware of many things: Wynette's sudden hostility, Barnes's reluctant sympathy, his own abject misery. Most of all, he was aware of the overwhelming fear that he'd lost her forever.

"What I want to know is who's got it in for her and why?" Wynette's entire body radiated cold fury. "That girl's never hurt anybody; she just doesn't have it in her."

"Herrera," Donovan told her, finding his voice again. "Her loving fiancé wants to kill her."

Barnes looked back and forth between them, obviously

confused. "Herrera?" he repeated. "Never heard of him. Santos is the one who hired me. León Santos."

Anna mindlessly watched the mile markers zip by, not thinking beyond putting as much distance as possible between herself and that hideous thug. He would have killed her; he would have killed Wynette.

Only now did she realize what true terror was. When she'd run away from Sonrisa, she'd told herself it was because she feared what 'Tavio might do to her. But that had been a meaningless concept with no substance, merely a silly, innocent woman's musings. If she'd really believed it then, she knew, this morning's events wouldn't have left her so numbed. Somewhere deep inside, a part of her had clung to the fantasy that, when all was said and done, 'Tavio wouldn't really hurt her.

But she knew the truth now; it gripped her with painful intensity. All her illusions about 'Tavio, every last one, had exploded to be replaced with an impersonal anger. It was as though he'd never existed for her except as a name she'd heard somewhere.

If only she could muster the same indifference toward Donovan, she thought. But his betrayal cut more deeply than any pain she'd ever known. She felt weak with nausea. It was almost like grief, she realized. She'd felt much the same way when Poppy died.

A blaring horn wrenched her back to the present, and she jerked the steering wheel to bring the Firebird back into the proper lane. *Time to stop*, she thought, *before I get someone killed*.

She recognized the irony; she endangered people's lives no matter what she did. Coming or going, Anna Michelotti was a public menace.

She pulled off the interstate at the next exit and found a motel. It wasn't the classiest place she'd ever seen, but at the moment she only wanted a dark room and clean sheets.

The disinterested desk clerk obtained her signature and

cash in advance, then passed her a key to room 22. "Third from the end, this side," he recited, and went back to watching an ancient episode of *My Three Sons* before she'd even left the counter.

Room 22 reflected her mood perfectly. It was drab and forlorn-looking. The drapes and bedspread were faded orange; everything else was washed-out tan.

Setting her suitcase down beside the bed, she sank onto the mattress.

Sooner or later she would have to make some decisions, find a place to go, call Wynette. But not yet. All she wanted to do now was sleep, and she didn't really care if she never woke up.

All the signs of deep depression, she noted with clinical detachment. She saw it every day in her work and had all the educated jargon to explain it to the students who came to her for counselling. But she had no desire to apply the same techniques to herself.

Oblivion was the only state she sought. Closing her eyes, she allowed herself to sink into it, welcoming the release.

Donovan hung up the phone with a bang.

"Felix can't reach his friend until tomorrow. Damn! She never really told me what she'd found out. How is Santos connected to Herrera?"

Wynette paced the floor. The bruise on her head had sprouted into a full fledged goose egg, making her look like the underdog in a roller derby. "She wouldn't tell me anything, except that she didn't want me involved."

"I can't help either," Barnes added. "Santos called me himself and he never mentioned anyone else."

"This is crazy! Wynette, are you sure she never mentioned anyone else she might go to, some place she'd feel safe?"

"Lord, you must think I'm stupid, askin' me a question like that! You think I haven't tried to come up with somethin'? She's been my friend for a long time, Donovan,

109

sometimes my only friend. She means more to me than you could ever understand."

"Don't be too sure of that, Wynette," he answered quietly.

Her expression softened. "Come on and sit down. She promised she'd call and she will."

The phone didn't ring until nearly dark. Wynette grabbed the receiver before Donovan could move.

"Yes? Oh, Anna, thank God! Listen, where are you?"

"I'm not sure," Anna told her. "A motel somewhere north of Los Angeles. I didn't pay any attention . . ."

"What's wrong? You sound funny."

Donovan moved to take the receiver, but Wynette waved him away.

"I just woke up," Anna was saying in a weak voice. "I'm still a little groggy."

"Anna, listen. You need to get back here, girl. You can't stay out there by yourself."

"Come back? Wyn, you know what happened this morning! You nearly got killed because of me."

"No, not to stay here," Wynette said impatiently. "To go back to Mexico with Donovan . . ."

Anna's gasp came through the line clearly. "Donovan? What's he doing there?"

Donovan couldn't wait any longer. He snatched the phone from Wynette's hand. "Anna, tell me where you are, I'll come get you . . ."

The line went dead and he stared, disbelieving, at the receiver. "She hung up."

Wynette began to cry. "Lord, what's gonna happen to her now?"

"Nothing," Donovan declared flatly. "Barnes, do you want in on this?"

"Sorry, Donovan." Barnes straightened his jacket and walked to the front door. "If Santos ever finds out I crossed him, I'm a dead man."

After he left, Donovan and Wynette looked at each other. Wynette's face was streaked with tears, Donovan's set in grim lines, emphasizing the harsh, angular planes.

"What do we do now, Donovan?"

His amber eyes were as cold as his voice. "You're going to stay here by the phone in case she calls again. I'm going back to Baja to find León Santos."

═══ 9 ═══

FELIX MET HIM at the Santa Marta airport. They didn't waste any time exchanging pleasantries.

"I found Santos for you," Felix said, taking Donovan's bag. "He works for Herrera, and for old Michelotti before that. Calls himself a business manager."

"And the trails leads right back to Herrera."

"Yeah. Couldn't locate much background on Santos, except that he hasn't led an unblemished life. No arrests or convictions, though." He pointed Donovan out the east entrance of the terminal. "Didn't have time to wait for the ferry, so I brought the chopper."

The glaring sun nearly obliterated the small hangars and charter service buildings, and Donovan squinted his eyes. Los Angeles had been overcast when he left, more in keeping with his general mood.

"Have you reached your friend the spy yet?"

"No, but I left a message. He'll be in touch as soon as he gets it. I don't think he has anything on Santos, or he'd have mentioned him to me."

Donovan let his skepticism show in a mocking smile, but he didn't say anything more about Felix's secretive friend. "So Santos is on Sonrisa. Why hasn't his name come up before now? I thought you'd been keeping up with the whole bunch for your friend."

"He's smart enough to keep a low profile, I guess. Most of his clout is secondhand, you know—he gives orders in Herrera's name, and Michelotti's before that. But there's some talk on the street that he's making a pitch to become a don in his own right."

Donovan's heels came down hard on the tarmac, punctuating his sarcasm. "A don, huh? Well, his career's about to hit a snag. We're going to the island."

Felix's jaw dropped. "You're out of your mind, Jay! Herrera would probably meet you with a firing squad. Even if you managed to get close to him, what are you going to do, walk in and say, 'Hey, *amigo*, you've been picking on my girl'?" He shook his head in disgust. "Get serious. If you confront him now, it'll blow the investigation, and I'll be in hot water like you wouldn't believe."

Donovan kept walking, faster now. "I'll keep you out of it, Felix. But I've got to do this."

"Keep me out of it?" Felix grabbed Donovan's arm and swung him around. "You're not listening to me, buddy. This is a government operation we're talking about . . ."

Donovan knocked his hand away. "You're the one who's not listening, *pal*. She managed to get away from Crewe yesterday, but he was right behind her, and who knows how many other goons Herrera's sent after her? To hell with your government operation! They're trying to *kill* her!"

Felix backed away, his features marked with frustration. "I know that, Jay. What I don't know is what to do about it . . ."

"Then we've got a real problem, because I know exactly what to do about it." He jerked his bag from Felix's hand and made for the helicopter again. "If you're not coming with me, you better start looking for another ride back to Guaymas."

"Jay, you can't take on Herrera by yourself. Just wait until I hear from Pete. We'll talk to him about it, work something out."

"You wait. I'm going in."

He threw his bag into the Huey and climbed in, leaving Felix to stand and stare. Not until the rotors were whirling did Felix relent.

When he was seated, he gave Donovan a cocky grin and a thumbs-up. "Can't let you be stupid by yourself," he yelled over the noise.

Donovan returned the sign, his anger gone. He'd always been able to count on Felix.

Both men donned headsets; Donovan requested and received clearance from the tower, then he put the chopper into motion. The land fell away, and he felt the old vitality surge through his veins, that special charge he got only when he was flying. He hoped the adrenalin would be enough to see him through what was coming.

During the flight, Donovan filled Felix in on all the details of the Laguna Beach scene and listened to the scant facts Felix had been able to piece together.

Some weeks earlier, Felix told him, the *federales* had attempted to stop two vans they suspected of hauling contraband. Gunfire was exchanged, and one of the officers, as well as their vehicle, was disabled. The vans headed for the desert and disappeared. Six days later, the *federales* stumbled on some bodies in the desert, nearly twenty of them.

"I remember the news reports," Donovan said. "They were illegals."

"Right. The vans weren't carrying drugs; they were loaded with people. Looks like they were dumped after the run-in with the cops," Felix said in disgust. "Anyway, it seems there was one survivor, a sixteen-year-old kid. He didn't know much, but what he did know led back here, to someone connected with the Michelottis. That's when Pete Tanner contacted me."

"And?"

"And nothing. That's where it is—stalemate. No proof, just suspicions."

"So that's why Tanner offered Anna protection. He thought she could wrap it up for him."

Felix shrugged. "Makes sense. And you've got to admit, it's the best thing she's got going for her."

"Maybe."

They made the rest of the flight in silence, until the island loomed before them, sparkling under the sun like a many-faceted emerald.

"Are you sure we can handle this?" Felix said as the copter settled into the sand.

"You've got a bad attitude, buddy." Donovan removed his headset and shot Felix an impish grin. "The question is, are they sure they can handle us?"

As they followed a path through tropical growth from the beach to the house, Donovan could almost imagine himself back in Southeast Asia, creeping through the undergrowth, expecting Charlie to drop on his neck from a tree. He turned often to check behind him.

Felix's rigid posture and darting eyes told Donovan that he felt the same, his nerve ends exposed.

In five minutes, they were at the house. The scene was tranquil, outwardly normal. There were no guards, only an old man tending a small ring of exotic-looking flowers that encircled a stone sundial. About fifty yards away stood a gazebo and, beyond it, a greenhouse.

"What now?" Felix asked.

"Let's try the front door," Donovan answered, "and see who answers."

"You're *loco*, Donovan." Felix looked as though he were ready to bolt and run. "It's not too late to change your mind, let Pete handle this."

Donovan made a rude suggestion concerning Pete and mounted the front steps. He banged the heavy, ornate knocker three times, then stepped back to wait.

The door opened almost immediately, and a plump, smiling woman looked at them inquiringly. "*Si?*" she said politely.

"We'd like to see *señor* Herrera," Donovan requested, equally polite.

"Please come in," she said in heavily accented English, opening the door wide.

The men entered warily, and she closed the door behind them. "I'll tell him you are here. *Señor* . . .?"

"Donovan."

She smiled again and left them alone in the large foyer, disappearing through a set of double doors near the staircase.

Donovan's first instinct was to charge through those doors and rip out Herrera's throat. He must have taken an automatic step in that direction, for Felix laid a restraining hand on his arm.

"Jay, something's not kosher. This was too easy." Felix's nervousness was obviously increasing with each passing second.

Donovan was inclined to agree with him. Even the most laid-back of criminals would have some security system, especially if he were being threatened with imminent exposure by a witness on the loose. Yet it seemed that anyone who came to Herrera's door had free access to his house as though he were, indeed, a legitimate businessman with nothing to hide. Definitely not kosher.

"What if we've made a mistake? I mean, what if Herrera's legit?"

Not bloody likely, Donovan thought. Aloud he merely said, "Then we'll find out soon, won't we?"

The plump woman reappeared and gestured to them. "*Señor* Herrera asks you to join him." She waited until they were inside the study, then left, unobtrusively closing the door.

A handsome, youngish man with a slight build rose from behind an antique oak desk and came forward to greet them with an outstretched hand. "Mr. Donovan?" His voice was pleasant and low-pitched. "I am Octavio Herrera. How can I help you?"

Donovan ignored the proffered hand, then took a step closer to Herrera while Felix flanked him. "Pretty sure of yourself, aren't you, Herrera?" he grated, his fists itching to make contact with the Mexican's too-perfect face.

Herrera's expression hardened as he looked from Donovan to Felix and back again. "I'm afraid I don't follow you," he said calmly.

"I'm talking about your hired hands. This their day off, or did you send them all to Laguna Beach?" Donovan took another step, but Herrera stood firm.

"I'm not very good at riddles, I'm afraid. If you care to explain, I'll be happy to listen. Otherwise . . ."

Donovan's control broke. Grabbing the lapels of Herrera's expensive suit coat with both hands, he jerked the man so close their faces nearly touched. "Don't push me, Herrera. I'm telling you to call off your dogs, right now." He took a childish pleasure in watching Herrera's nonchalance turn into fear. "Whatever it takes, you get in touch with Crewe and Santos and anyone else you sent after her and call—them—off." He punctuated each of his last words with a hard shake.

Then he felt something hard prod his stomach. "You will release me now, Mr. Donovan, or I will surely shoot you." Herrera nudged the gun, not gently, for emphasis.

Beside him, Donovan heard Felix groan. "I knew it was too easy."

Donovan let his hands fall away, cursing himself for a hotheaded fool. The gun pointed at his belly seemed to stimulate his imagination, and now, too late, he thought of a half dozen ways they could have gotten the drop on Herrera.

"Fortunately for you, Mr. Donovan, you have mentioned two names that interest me greatly. That is the only reason you are not in a great deal of pain." With his free hand, Herrera indicated two chairs near the oak desk. "Take a seat, gentlemen. It appears we have something to discuss."

Through the windshield, Anna stared helplessly at the highway. Every red light on the Firebird's dash seemed to be glowing, mocking her ignorance. She hadn't the slightest idea what might be wrong; the car had shuddered and died and now refused to be resurrected.

Maybe if she raised the hood, she'd see something obvious. Admittedly it was a long shot, but it was the best idea she could come up with.

After a few minutes fumbling, she figured out the mechanism and popped up the hood. Other than an unfamiliar smell, she noticed nothing out of place.

Great, she thought, *just what I need.* She felt like crying but decided she'd done enough of that in the last twelve hours. If she didn't get a grip on herself and her situation soon, it might be too late. For all she knew, that gangster, or one of his buddies, might be only a step behind her. Worse, it could be Jay Donovan. As soon as the thought materialized, she condemned it as paranoid. If they were that close, they'd have taken her at the motel yesterday.

Still, she felt frighteningly exposed, just standing on the side of the highway. It was at least five miles back to San Luis Obispo, and she wasn't sure what was ahead. Mostly small farming communities, she thought, and she didn't know how far the next one was. Probably closer than going back, but she really wasn't willing to take the chance.

She was hanging over the seat, fishing in her suitcase for a pair of shoes more suited to walking than the low-heeled pumps she wore, when a whoosh of airbrakes sounded behind the Firebird. She looked out the back window into the shiny chrome grill of a GMC truck. Scrambling outside, she squared her shoulders and prepared to meet the truck driver with no trace of the fear she felt.

He was a young man—probably older than he looked or he wouldn't be driving—but to Anna he looked like a kid and she felt herself relax. Surely freckles and a cowlick qualified him as one of the good guys, she thought, then immediately regretted the frivolity. How many times would she have to be dumped on before she quit trusting people?

The very young man patted the rear fender of the Firebird as he passed. "Nice car when she's runnin', huh?"

Anna laughed nervously. "You've got that right. It just quit, very nicely, of course."

"Lemme look at it. Might be somethin' I can fix for ya." Without waiting for permission, he stuck his top half under the hood. Anna thought irreverently that his low-riding jeans would look much better without the Fruit of the Loom elastic waistband as gilding.

A few minutes later he emerged, wiping his hands on his faded jeans. "Looks like the water pump, lady."

"Well, can you fix it?" she asked hopefully.

"Naw." He seemed slightly amused that she had asked. "You'll either have to get that one rebuilt or buy a new one."

"Oh." She gnawed at her bottom lip. "Are they very expensive?"

He shrugged. "Depends."

On what? she wanted to scream. "Oh," she said again.

"Look, I can give you a lift if you want. There's a garage in Atascadero."

She thought it over for five seconds before deciding that she really had no viable options. "Okay, thanks. I'll get my purse."

Atascadero did indeed have a garage. Apparently it was the only one for a couple hundred miles, judging from the piles of cars that ringed it.

Anna patiently explained to the mechanic, whose stitched coverall pocket identified him as Mitch, that she needed a water pump and someone to install it. Just as patiently, Mitch explained to Anna that he ran a one-man business and couldn't leave his other work.

"Then can I get it towed in?"

"Not from here. Might get somebody from San Luis Obispo."

"If I can get it here, can you fix it?"

"Not today." He spat on the ground. "Maybe tomorrow."

Defeated, she walked back to the waiting truck driver. "Dead end, Gene."

"Yeah, I heard. Whatcha gonna do?"

She sighed. "I wish I knew."

"Listen, if you're headed somewhere on my route, why not ride along with me? Then you could get your husband or your boyfriend or whoever to come back and take care of things."

Anna tried not to smile. It had been a long time since she encountered such youthful earnestness. "I don't think so, Gene, but thanks for the offer."

"Okay, so what *are* you gonna do? I can drop you at a motel."

She closed her eyes. This was all so complicated. Why not go with Gene? She had nowhere else to go, not really. Her only plans, half-cocked as they were, had been to drive to San Jose and look up her college roommate. Maybe Gene's suggestion made sense. Unless 'Tavio or Donovan took a sudden notion to stop every eighteen-wheeler on the highway, she should be safe enough.

"Gene, where are you going from here?"

"I'm dropping this load in Oakland," he answered eagerly, "then I'll pick up another one in Sacramento going to Klamath Falls. If there's something ready there, I'll bring it back down to L.A."

"Look, I really don't have to be anywhere special, and I've always thought it might be fun to see the country from the cab of a truck. I can pay my own expenses."

"That's great!" His face fell. "But what about your car?"

"I'll take care of it, have it towed in."

"That's great!" he said again. "Looks like I got myself a partner."

"Santos has made a grave error in judgment," Herrera said coldly. "It will be his last mistake." He reached for the telephone, quickly dialed a number. "This is Herrera," he said after a few moments' wait. "I understand one of your field agents, Pete Tanner, is conducting an investigation of me . . . Never mind that, it's of no importance. You cannot prove what isn't true. I'm calling to bargain with you. I will give you your smuggler in return for a small favor . . . That is your option, of course. I hope you have thought of the consequences . . . This is not a threat, *señor*, it is a statement of fact. Not only will you lose your smuggler, you will be liable for explaining why American agents are working in Mexico without sanction . . . *Bueno*. There is a young woman named Anna Michelotti. I wish you to alert every law enforcement agency in California, Oregon, Nevada, and Arizona. This woman will be taken into custody soon. She is to be held in custody, and I am to be notified immediately . . ."

Donovan listened with growing respect, and at last a seed of hope began to grow. With Herrera's help, they had a real chance.

The conversation terminated, Herrera turned to Donovan and Ortiz once more. "Donovan, I would like you to call Anna's friend—Wynette?—and persuade her to report her automobile as stolen. Anna will be safe behind bars until one of us can get to her."

"Then we should get back to California as soon as possible," Donovan said, rising.

"That is no problem. We have a Sikorsky hangared at Santa Marta. Take it. It's outfitted with extra fuel tanks. It will make the trip easily and more quickly."

"Aren't you coming with us?" Felix asked.

"There are some loose ends to tie up here, such as locating Santos. He left yesterday afternoon, presumably after hearing from Crewe. I think he has gone to California to take care of Anna himself." He smiled grimly. "I've found that telephones can be most effective weapons when used properly. Besides, I feel my presence is really unnecessary, now that Mr. Donovan is on the scene."

He rose from the desk chair and offered his hand first to Felix and then to Donovan. This time Donovan accepted it.

In another room, next to the study where the three men had been closeted, a young woman clasped her hands together, torn by indecision. She didn't understand everything she'd overheard, but she knew *señor* Santos would want to know.

A tear slid down her cheek. Santos was a hard man, and she had never liked him, but she had obligations. She had accepted his money and the responsibility that came with it. Besides, she was too afraid to disobey him; one heard stories of how he repaid disloyalty.

Reluctantly she withdrew a piece of paper from her apron pocket and unfolded it. This was the number she was to use to contact him, and she must only use the special telephone, the one he had shown her before he left. *Dios mío*, she prayed, *let me be doing the right thing*.

— 10 —

THE JUKE BOX was too loud and so were the customers, but to Anna, the truck stop was heavenly. Nearly faint with hunger, she let Gene lead her to a booth in an alcove marked with a hand-lettered sign, Truckers Only. The mingled aromas of fried hamburger, onions, and coffee made her mouth water.

"This is it," Gene said happily, sliding into the seat facing her. "Best chicken-fried steak anywhere outside of Texas."

"Then that's what I'll have, a big one with lots of gravy." She looked at the pastry cooler behind the long counter. "And strawberry pie for dessert."

Gene looked at her in surprise. "Boy, I sure wouldn't have taken you for a big eater, you're so . . ."

"Skinny?" she prompted, smiling.

"No! You're—you're elegant." He blushed, a deep red that hid his freckles. "I think you're beautiful."

The arrival of the waitress saved him from any more embarrassing revelations, and after they placed their order, Anna carefully kept the conversation as impersonal as possible.

Gene was fun to talk to, full of enthusiasm and optimism. He responded to her attention like a puppy, so it was easy to keep him busy answering her questions. He was from Denton, Texas, she learned, and driving was his lifelong dream, ever since he used to spend the summers riding along with his father. "Boy, has he got a great rig.

You'd really like him, Anna. He financed my truck for me so I could go independent. You have to be twenty-five to be a company driver, see, because of the insurance, but I didn't wanna wait that long . . ."

Anna tried to pay attention, but her mind kept drifting away. Now that the shock and terror were past, she could think about Donovan without going to pieces. She wasn't pleased with her thoughts, for she was right back where she started, vacillating between two extremes. Had he betrayed her or hadn't he? Could she trust him or couldn't she? Did she love him or didn't she?

". . . where'd you go? Anna?"

Her eyes focused on Gene's sweet face, so worried and concerned. "Oh. I'm sorry, Gene. I didn't mean to be rude. I was just thinking." Her plate, which she only vaguely remembered being set before her, was half-empty. "You were right. This is the best chicken-fried steak I've ever tasted."

"Yeah, I knew you'd like it," he beamed. "So what were you thinkin' about? You looked mighty serious."

"Just trying to work out some problems. That's why I decided to take this vacation, you know. Sometimes it helps to put some distance between yourself and the things that worry you."

Gene nodded wisely. "Know whatcha mean. Seems like I do my best thinkin' when it's just me and my truck, rollin' along." He pushed his plate back. "Guess we better get to it."

"Do you mind if I stop in the western store and buy a change of clothes?" She'd noticed the shop as they entered the restaurant, right in the same building.

"Sure, no problem. I can get my boots shined while you shop."

She waited while Gene paid the tab. As they turned away from the cash register, a tall man pushed by, jostling her roughly. She stumbled against Gene, who caught her and cursed, the first time she'd heard him say anything that wasn't polite.

"Damn bikers. I oughta . . ."

She caught his arm. "No, it's okay. I don't think he meant to." Actually she thought just the opposite, but the man and his friends, four in all, didn't strike her as the type to take any lip from someone like Gene. If she were casting a movie about dirty, sullen, troublemaking punks, they would have been the first choices. Leather jackets, bandannas, and beards—they had it all.

As they passed, the man in the lead looked at Anna with insolent boldness, making her want to cringe.

Gene saw the leer and cursed again. "Let's go, Gene," she said quickly. "I don't want any trouble."

Ten minutes later she was waiting for her purchases to be bagged, wondering if she should have picked up a sweater along with the jeans and shirt. It was much cooler here than in L.A., and if she went as far as Oregon . . .

"Hey, pretty lady, where's your boyfriend?"

Whirling, she found herself facing the bikers; her stomach sank.

The clerk, a hard-looking older woman, spoke sharply. "Unless you want to buy something, buddy, move on out and leave her alone." She thrust a bag toward Anna. "Here you go, honey. Don't forget your change."

"Yes . . . thank you." Anna dropped several bills and coins into the sack, then took a step toward the door.

"Aw, don't be unfriendly." The man's teeth were even and white, but his mouth was cruel. His jacket didn't quite hide the black T-shirt with the filthy slogan printed in silver letters. He was at least forty, Anna thought.

"Come on, let me buy you something. How about a room for the night?" He looked at his friends for approval, and they dutifully laughed.

Anna clutched the bag tightly. "Aren't you a little old to be playing games?"

"Games? I'm as serious as a heart attack, honey. I really dig the way you—"

One of the other bikers nudged him, gesturing with his thumb.

Anna looked past them. Gene, flanked by several drivers she'd noticed in the restaurant, had entered the store. Now they stood unmoving, blocking the exit, all of them stoney faced, all of them big.

She heard the store clerk gasp. "Hey, guys, give me a break, okay? Take it outside."

"Come on, Anna," Gene ordered, not raising his voice. "Go on out to the truck."

She started to obey but found her arm firmly caught in the biker's grip. "I say she stays, junior. Let her see what happens to snot-noses like you—"

That was the last coherent word out of his mouth. Gene dived for the biker, the other truckers close on his heels. Anna felt her sleeve rip and she was knocked aside. Through the sound of fists hitting faces, grunts, curses, and scuffling boots, the clerk yelled, "Somebody call the cops!"

"Stop it! Stop it!" she screamed, but if anyone heard her, they chose to ignore it.

Someone fell against a display cabinet, and it toppled over with a crash, sending jewelry and glass flying through the air.

The clerk crawled over the counter and gave her a shove. "Come on, honey, somebody's fixing to get killed!" Dodging the wild punches and reeling bodies, the two women skirted the fight and made it to the door.

Then Anna looked back, just in time to see Gene go down. A square-toed boot caught him in the ribs, and he arched convulsively. Dropping the sack, she darted into the fracas, fighting her way to Gene's aid. Something struck her between the shoulder blades, and she sprawled on the floor, dazed and breathless. But Gene was right there, and she managed to cover his body with her own. She tensed, waiting for a blow.

"Stupid broad." Rough hands grasped her waist, hauled her up. She kicked out, connected with someone, fell. The hands were on her again and she flailed wildly. Then something cold bit into her wrist, clicked.

She looked up into the unamused face of a clean-shaven, khaki-shirted man. On his head perched a hat adorned with an emblem that read Salinas Police Department. "Let's go, lady. You're under arrest."

"I don't understand," Wynette said, uncrossing her long legs to lean forward on the sofa, elbows on knees. "If Santos is doin' somethin' illegal with the mines, why didn't 'Tavio pull his plug? Then none of this would've happened, Anna would be safe, and we wouldn't all be sittin' around here like idiots, lookin' at each other and waitin' for the phone to ring."

"Because Herrera didn't know; he only suspected. He was looking for proof. Now he's found it." The coffee cup in Felix's hand was empty, and now he set it beside the two other empty ones on the end table.

"That doesn't tell me doodly," Wynette retorted. "How does smugglin' people to the States tie in with stealin' from the mines?"

"It's just a theory, Wynette, but it makes sense," Donovan explained from across the room, where he stood looking out the window. He and Felix had discussed it at length with Herrera before they left Mexico. Then, during the long flight up the coast of Baja and into California, he and Felix had enlarged upon the theory, refining it. "Part of Herrera's problem was that he couldn't find a single person who'd actually worked in any of the mines. All he had was the mention of Santos's name in an ore transaction.

"So, what if Santos had married the two operations? He brings in the illegals to work the mines, then transports both them and the ore across the border. There's always a fresh supply of workers, no payroll records, and everybody gets what they want."

"Except the ones who get dumped in the desert," Wynette said.

"Yeah. And the ones like Anna, who get in the way." So far, Donovan had managed to keep his frustration under control, but now he could feel it getting the upper hand again. Part of him wanted to maintain the cool facade; another part wanted to rant, break furniture, knock down a few walls. "Why the *hell* haven't we heard something!"

"Because she's smart, Donovan," Wynette told him. "She's takin' care of herself, stayin' out of sight."

"Maybe." He shook a cigarette out of the pack. "And maybe Santos already has her." He put the cigarette between his lips, then removed it, broke it in two and flung the pieces away.

Wynette went to him and put her arms around his shoulders. "I love her too, Donovan."

He clasped her hard, and they held each other for a moment.

The phone rang, startlingly loud in the silence that had fallen, and they sprang apart. Wynette grabbed the receiver before it could ring a second time.

"Yes? This is she . . . Where?" She plopped on the sofa again, as if she were suddenly too tired to stand. "Did you hear her say where she was goin'? All right, thank you. I'll pick it up tomorrow.

"Well, as of yesterday morning, she was all right," Wynette said, replacing the receiver. "The car broke down; it's at a garage in Atascadero. She was with a truck driver. The mechanic said she left my name and number and told him to call me when the car was towed in."

"She left with the trucker?" Felix broke into laughter while Wyn and Donovan glared at him. "That's great! She is one smart lady. Santos will never find her." He laughed again. "Relax, Jay. She's safe, don't you understand? Maybe you don't have her, but neither do they."

Almost reluctantly, Wynette joined in. "He's got a point, Donovan. She's got bad guys, good guys, and cops lookin' for her, and she's hidin' in a truck." She whooped. "Can you see her, all kicked back, listenin' to Merle Haggard? Lord, she's probably havin' the time of her life."

"Clowns, both of you," Donovan growled. "She may not be any safer with that trucker than she would be with Santos. And she'll never be safe from him until he's put away."

Felix and Wynette sobered. "Look, Jay," Felix said, "it's a tough situation having to just wait around like this, but you have to admit it's nice to know she's all right, even if you don't know where she is."

"But maybe we can find out," Wynette said, her eyes sparkling with excitement. "Why don't we talk to the mechanic at the garage where she stopped? Maybe he knows more than he thinks."

Felix nodded. "Not a bad idea. There could have been a name on the truck, and we could trace it."

"Okay, let's call." Donovan was grateful for any excuse to do something constructive. "It's a long shot, but worth a try."

"Can't call," Wynette told them. "I didn't think to get the name of the garage. But we could drive up there. He said it's the only garage in town."

"I'm not going anywhere except to pick Anna up."

"You stay here, then. Felix and I can go. I have to pick up the car anyway."

"Okay, why not? It'll get you two hyenas out of my hair. But call when you get there."

"How far is it?" Felix wanted to know.

"Four or five hours at least," Wyn replied. "It's ten now. We should be there by two or three, and back here no later than midnight."

"And who knows, maybe we'll get lucky and bring her back with us."

"Maybe." But Donovan had learned long ago never to trust in luck.

After Felix and Wynette left, with much good-natured bickering and joking, Donovan felt at loose ends. He missed their reassurances, the camaraderie that had kept them all bolstered up throughout the long hours of uncertainty. Two weeks ago he would have told anyone who asked that he preferred being alone. Now he was burdened by isolation, his nerves stretched almost to the breaking point.

Part of his trouble, he knew, was plain old tiredness. The flight up from Baja was long and grueling. They hadn't arrived at Wynette's until well after midnight, and of course she had wanted to hear everything. In all, he had missed enough sleep during the past week to turn him into a zombie.

Maybe now would be a good time to catch up on some of the backlog, he thought. The phone was right here, so he wouldn't miss any calls. He slipped off his shoes, took off his shirt and hung it over the lamp shade. Then he stretched out on the floor, cushioned by the large, colorful pillows Wynette seemed to be so fond of.

His eyes closed, and almost instantly he felt himself slipping away into that state of utter clarity that sometimes preceded sleep, when he understood so many things that eluded his waking self. Now he realized that a memory of Fleur had been teasing at his consciousness for days, but it had never been able to fully materialize.

He could see her, almost imagine she was there. Her delicate face, wide-eyed and smiling, seemed to hover above him, as though she were trying to tell him something.

Then the memory became clear. Fleur had been telling him about her mother's death and her father's serene acceptance of his loss. "He knew they would meet again, as they have before," she said, holding his hand. "He had not lost her forever."

"Do you really believe that? Reincarnation?" He laughed, not cruelly. "Come on, honey, that's a fairy tale."

"But it is true, Dahno-Vahn," she said seriously. "Each person has another half, someone to complete the circle.

You will understand one day, and remember that you laughed at me." Her tiny hands touched his face. "You care for me, Dahno-Vahn, but I do not complete you. When you meet her, you will know. She will be a stranger, yet you have known her forever. You will know what is in her soul . . ."

You were right, Fleur. I do understand now. Thank you.

He said good-bye to her and fell into normal sleep. He wanted to tell Anna, make her understand. And he would. He would find her, and when he did, he would never lose her again.

Anna thought the six-by-eight cell was the most hideously depressing place she'd ever seen. There were no windows, only the bars that comprised one of the four walls. The other three were of gray cinder block, and the floor was gray concrete.

The bunk where she sat was small and uncomfortable; at least the sheet and blanket were clean, but so thin from repeated washings she could probably tear them with a fingernail. There were two patches of white to relieve the institutional monochrome—the toilet stool, which stood in plain sight of anyone walking past, and a rust-stained lavatory bolted to the back wall.

The ultimate security, she sighed inwardly. It was easy to understand how someone would choose to die rather than spend their life behind bars. She yearned for Sonrisa with a longing so intense it blotted out everything else. If she closed her eyes and concentrated, she could hear the surf, feel the wind lifting her hair from her neck. And the smell—ocean and flowers mingled in a heady aroma . . .

Step now, Anna; feel the sand beneath your feet, between your toes. This is Sonrisa and someday it will be yours.

Remembering, she smiled. It had been her birthday, the first after her parents had died. Poppy had made her a gift of the island, spending hours showing her the plants, seashells, letting her play in the cove until she fell asleep in the sand. Thereafter, she'd considered the island hers, never doubting that she would spend her life there.

Soon, she thought vehemently, *soon I'll go back, and everything will be beautiful again.*

Footsteps echoed off the walls, breaking into her reverie, and seconds later the jailer appeared with a tray of food.

"Room service," he sang out. "The blue plate special, 'specially for you." He slid the tray through the oblong opening. "You feeling better?"

"Better than what?" Anna mocked. She took the tray and sat down again, balancing it across her lap. "How much longer do I have to stay here?"

"Guess it depends on what we find out," he answered. "We're checking wants and warrants now. If you come out clean, then you can leave."

"What happened to Gene? He was hurt in the fight."

"If you mean the young trucker, I heard they took him to the hospital. He's a little banged up, but it's nothing fatal." He smiled at her almost kindly, and she was reassured.

"What about the others?"

"The truckers paid their fines and left. That other bunch is in the next hall. The store manager filed charges, so they'll be held over for arraignment." She must have let her sudden apprehension show, for he said, "Don't worry, you won't have to see them. We put them in the deluxe suite. Eat your lunch before it gets cold. I'll be back later for the tray."

He left her looking doubtfully at the unidentifiable food on the tray. Back in the day room, he remarked, "She shouldn't be in there, a nice girl like that. Wonder what her story is?"

"I've been wondering the same thing," said his co-worker. "No ID, nobody to vouch for her. Maybe she's a runaway wife."

A third person entered the room, a tall woman holding a sheet of paper. "Well, you can both stop wondering. This just came through." She passed the sheet to the jailer; he looked at it and whistled, showed it to the other man.

"Auto theft."

"You missed the most important part, dummy. It's flagged."

"Government? Jeez, you don't see too many of those. Think maybe she's a terrorist?"

"Whatever she is, it's not our problem," the woman said, retrieving the sheet. "I've got to make that call. Want to bet she's out of here by tonight?"

Herrera took the call in the study. In the adjacent room, a trembling hand carefully lifted the receiver of the extension telephone. The woman listened, not daring to breathe.

The conversation was brief but explicit.

This is what señor *Santos wants to know,* she thought, nervous to the point of nausea. She would call him immediately, pass on the information. Then, please God, her part would be finished and not soon enough.

It would be difficult to stay here, knowing she had betrayed *señor* Herrera, but what choice had she? He might dismiss her if he found out, but Santos would do much worse.

And *señorita* Anna. What trouble was she in, to be in jail? The woman crossed herself and hurried from the room.

— 11 —

THE CALL CAME a little after four o'clock. The phone rang several times before Donovan shook the sleep away and remembered where he was.

Herrera's voice came clearly over the line, sounding like he was next door rather than eight hundred miles away.

"She's in Salinas, the city jail," Herrera said. "I've already made the necessary arrangements. A police car will meet you at the municipal airport north of the city and turn her over to you."

"Won't I need some kind of authorization?" His head hurt from too little rest, and the ribs Crewe worked on had begun to pain him again.

"No, you need nothing but to be there. How far are you from Salinas?"

Donovan tried to think, but he was groggy and unfamiliar with this part of the country. "At least several hours by air, maybe more."

"It will work out all right, then. I told them ten o'clock tonight." Herrera paused. "Donovan, don't relax. I haven't located Santos, and I think he may have been warned away. If he knows, he'll be more dangerous than ever."

"I'll be careful. We'll have to stop at San Diego for refueling, then it'll be a straight shot from there."

"Donovan, there's one more thing for you to consider. If you allow anything to happen to her, I will probably try to kill you."

Donovan laughed without humor. "And I will probably not blame you. We'll see you sometime tomorrow."

He pulled on his shirt and shoes quickly, but he resented every minute. He should have been dressed and waiting, he shouldn't have gone to sleep, he shouldn't have let her go in the first place.

More precious time was lost while he called the flight service station, listened to the prerecorded message. *No weather problems*, he thought gratefully; one less thing to worry about. Now if he could only get through to file his flight plan . . . He tried the number three times and gave up in disgust, unable to get past the busy signal. Slamming down the receiver, he strode toward the front door. He'd just have to file from the air.

His hand was on the doorknob when he remembered Wynette and Felix. They hadn't called yet, but he couldn't afford to wait. In the kitchen, he scrabbled in the drawers until he found a pencil and a small paper bag. The note, when he finished it, was barely legible, but it would have to do. He propped it against the coffee pot and ran out of the apartment.

He'd left the Sikorsky at a private airstrip near San Juan Capistrano, courtesy of another of Herrera's contacts. When they'd landed late last night, the owner had met them personally, given them the keys to his car and told them to call him day or night if they needed anything. He wondered what kind of pull Herrera had that would make people smile while they were being imposed upon. Whatever it was, it sure as hell came in handy.

The man was there again when Donovan arrived, smiling and polite, wishing Donovan the best of luck. He repossessed his keys, shook Donovan's hand and left. Not once, Donovan realized, had the man asked a single question or betrayed any curiosity. Apparently Herrera had impressed upon him that his was not a need-to-know situation.

Thank God for the Sikorsky, Donovan thought for the hundredth time. The Sikorsky was faster, safer, more maneuverable, altogether a superior machine. Donovan loved it. Maybe someday he'd have one of his own, and he would teach Anna to fly . . .

Anna. He hadn't cried for years, but it would be easy to do so now. She was safe; he would see her soon, and the relief was nearly overwhelming. Not until this moment did he realize that he had never really faced the possibility of losing her. The thought had simply been too painful to contemplate. If he lost Anna, he lost himself.

Automatically he went through the preflight check, found the Salinas airport on his chart, noted the coordinates. Over four hundred nautical miles, he calculated. A long haul but not as far as he'd feared. He had plenty of time.

Then he was airborne, sailing toward Salinas and Anna.

In San Francisco, another man was also savoring the thought of reaching Salinas and Anna Michelotti.

León Santos congratulated himself on his foresight. He had almost sent Crewe to San Francisco while he himself stayed in Los Angeles. Perhaps it was precognition, he thought, that he had changed his plans at the last moment. Now he was much closer to his quarry than that fool Donovan. He, Santos, would get there first, and he would make certain Donovan didn't live to interfere further in his plans.

There were only a few more details to arrange, and then he could leave. Lifting the telephone receiver, he dialed the number of a hotel room in Los Angeles. Crewe answered on the first ring.

"The woman is in Salinas. Your friend Donovan will pick her up at ten o'clock, and I will be there to meet them. I will drive on to Tijuana and hand her over to you at the place we discussed earlier, then I must leave. Arrange transportation to take her to the mine."

"No problem. But where will you be? I mean, what do you want me to do with her?"

"Exactly what I tell you to do with her, Crewe. Take her

to the mine, nothing more. I will attend to her personally, in my own good time."

"Sure, whatever you say."

Santos terminated the conversation abruptly. He had no patience with imbeciles, yet it seemed that he was continually forced to deal with men like Crewe. But no more, he promised himself. When this was over and he had proven to *El Patrón* that he could be trusted to handle any situation, he could, as the Americans said, write his own ticket.

It was only a matter of time before his empire surpassed that of Don Roberto's. But unlike that foolish old man, he would never throw away the power he gained. Only death would break his rule.

The magazine was two years old and dog-eared from use, but Anna was grateful to have something to relieve her boredom. She'd been through the words of every song she knew and was chagrined to realize there were so few. There had been a time when she could belt out every hit the disc jockeys played. Then she had tried to wear herself out with calisthenics, but she had found push-ups and deep knee bends to be as boring as ever. She had forced herself to take a nap, and that had provided the only interesting point in an otherwise pointless day.

Just before she woke, Donovan had seemed to be in the cell with her, trying to tell her something very important, but she hadn't been able to make out the words. His voice had sounded as though it were being channelled through a broken audio system set at minimum volume. She had realized, in the dream, that what he had to say was profound and somehow meaningful to her, and she kept trying to tell him that she couldn't understand. Then she came awake, to find that it was still today and she still didn't know what was going to happen to her.

When the jailer had come back to pick up her lunch tray, she tried to question him, but his earlier friendliness had vanished. He hadn't been rude, just withdrawn, and all he would say was that she'd be notified when a decision was made. As though she were a job applicant, she thought, trying to find some humor in her situation.

Later he had returned with several magazines, and she had gone through them all quickly. Now she was on the second read of the last one; when it was done, she'd be back to counting cinder blocks.

She heard the jailer returning, probably with her dinner. It was easy to lose track of time inside a cell, but she judged that lunch had been five or six hours before.

But he wasn't bringing her tray; he carried her shopping bag from the western store, and he had someone with him, a woman who was also in uniform. She was tall and dark-haired, somewhat older than Anna, but still on the early side of forty.

The woman smiled nervously—an odd reaction, Anna thought. In fact, it was another in a series of oddities. The first stirrings of unease sent her scooting back on the hard bunk, until her back was firmly against the cold wall.

"Miss Michelotti? I'm Officer Davis. The store clerk out at the truck stop told us you had paid for these clothes. I thought you might want to shower and change before you eat."

Anna stared at her. "I beg your pardon?"

"I said I thought you . . ."

"I heard what you said." Anna told herself it would be a mistake to antagonize the police, but frustration had finally gotten the upper hand. "I've been in these rags since yesterday. Don't tell me you just got around to noticing. Now, what's going on?"

The jailer cleared his throat. "Well, the fact is, you're going to be transferred out later tonight. It's standard policy to see that the inmates are cleaned up before they leave."

"Transferred? Where?" The uneasiness was quickly replaced by apprehension. "Just a little while ago, you told me the reports hadn't come back yet. And if they have come back, then you know I haven't done anything."

Officer Davis had stopped smiling. "As a matter of fact,

we got the report shortly after noon today. You're wanted for stealing a car, Miss Michelotti, and under ordinary circumstances you'd be held over."

Anna stood up then, her pulse throbbing wildly. "Then you're telling me this 'transfer' is not an ordinary circumstance."

"I'm not telling you anything except what I've already said. We're not holding you for the auto theft because there was a flag on your file. Arrangements have been made for your transfer out. Now, since you have to leave, wouldn't you rather leave clean?"

This is what it's like to walk the last mile, she thought as she was escorted out of her cell and down a wide corridor to the showers. It had to be 'Tavio. Somehow he'd convinced Wynette to swear out a warrant, and now she was being handed to him like a birthday present.

The jailer left the two women at the door to the bath, and Officer Davis silently watched her undress, showed her how to adjust the water. Then she stood under the spray, wishing she could wash away the dread that clutched at her like a vise.

After she dressed, the other woman produced a comb. Anna slowly worked the tangles out of her hair and neatly fixed it into her customary French braid. Her reflection was pale; not one spot of color relieved the whiteness of her face.

She was a fool, she decided suddenly. She'd been silent too long, and all the reasons were now invalid. Whether anyone believed her or not, telling her story would take time, and maybe someone would listen.

"I want to talk to whoever's in charge," she told Officer Davis. "I have knowledge of a crime, and I want to report it."

The other woman raised her eyebrows. "Local or f eral?"

"Federal. Illegal aliens."

"Well, that answers a few questions," Officer Davis said.

"We've all been wondering what the feds want with you. You must be a pretty important witness. We were told to give you the VIP treatment." She smiled, really smiled, for the first time. "Save it, honey. In a little while you can tell it to the top dogs."

Anna hugged the comment to her, wanting to sing with joy. The government! Then Donovan was telling the truth when he said she'd been protected as a material witness. It wasn't 'Tavio at all!

Almost happily, she went back to her cell with a much lighter step than when she'd left it.

Waiting, waiting, always waiting for Anna.

Donovan was too early; it was only nine o'clock, and he didn't know how he'd get through the next hour. If he could do what he wanted, he'd storm the police station and take her by force. But for now it was Herrera's show, so he'd observe the rules, galling as they might be.

He could check out the terminal, see if he could find something to eat. His last meal had been early that morning at Wynette's, and his stomach was beginning to protest. No, he decided. He was at the far end of the runway, and it was a long walk to the terminal. If the police got there early, he might not be back in time to see them arrive.

He lit another Camel, walked around the helicopter again. Maybe he should have chosen another spot, somewhere with better lighting, but he'd instinctively decided on the most remote place he could find. A holdover from his combat training, he supposed. Always give yourself the advantage, make the enemy expose themselves to get to you.

A faint rustle arrested his attention. He flipped the cigarette away and walked ten yards beyond the Sikorsky, straining to see into the darkness. There was nothing there, of course—no buildings, no trees, nothing for concealment. Still, just to make sure, he patrolled a wide circle, but he heard nothing more.

Nerves, Donovan, it's just nerves. Relax. This time you've got the jump on Santos.

The familiar sound of echoing footsteps alerted Anna that it was time to go. She'd been on edge for hours, anticipating her release, looking forward to the end of her ordeal. Maybe Donovan would be with the government people and she'd have a chance to tell him all the things she'd stored up.

Officer Davis opened the cell door, while two other men in plainclothes quietly waited.

"Here's your purse. We'd like you to check and make sure you've got everything."

Anna dug through the contents quickly, mostly to satisfy the requirements. She was so excited she wouldn't notice if anything were missing. "Yes, it's all here."

"Fine. These men are detectives. They're going to drive you out to the airport. You'll be met there. Good luck."

Anna left the cell without looking back. There was absolutely nothing in there she wanted to remember.

The ride through the streets of Salinas and out to the airport was the longest she'd ever taken. She sat in the front seat between the two men, hearing their occasional comments, but she paid no attention. Her thoughts were too full of the future to allow for any other intrusions.

They would live on Sonrisa, she and Jay; he would love it as much as she did. They would travel, see the world. He could work if he liked, maybe the charter service with his friend Felix. She had always wanted to start a school for problem children, and what better place for it than the island? And someday they'd have children of their own who would run and play on the beach, as full of happiness as she'd been.

When the airport came into sight, she edged forward on the seat. It was too dark to see much, but she tried anyway. Then they were actually driving on the runway, right for the very end, and she could see a helicopter. Jay, it had to be Jay!

Then he stepped out of the shadows into the glare of the headlights. Almost before the car doors were opened, she was pushing out of the seat past the detective.

Donovan opened his arms and she ran into them. "It's you," she sobbed, "it's really you!"

"I told you to trust me, sweetheart." He kissed her and she felt like flying.

"Well, I guess we can consider this an official transfer," said one of the detectives, grinning at them. "No need for us to stick around."

Anna and Donovan watched the car reverse and drive away, still holding on to each other.

"Oh, Jay, I've got so much to tell you. I thought you were mixed up with 'Tavio. That man said—"

"Let's wait until we're off the ground, honey. I've got a lot to tell you too, but we've got to get moving."

A figure stepped into the open, out of the shadows behind the Sikorsky.

"My sentiments exactly, Mr. Donovan," Santos said, raising a revolver. It spit three bullets through the silencer.

Anna saw the flashes, heard the ridiculously quiet pings, saw Donovan spin and fall. But it wasn't real, it couldn't be real, not now.

She kneeled beside his body and touched his shoulder. "Jay?" she said questioningly. "Jay, get up, we have to leave now."

Beside her, a man spoke. "He won't be coming with us, *señorita*."

She looked up into his dark, even-featured face. Though she couldn't see him clearly, she recognized his voice. "Santos?"

Something bit into her arm and she went to sleep.

═══ 12 ═══

SHE CAME TO her senses slowly, slipping in and out of consciousness over and over. Each time she held on to awareness a little longer, certain that it was imperative for her to wake up. Vaguely she thought she must be late for work; why hadn't the alarm gone off?

At last she could open her eyes.

In the semi-gloom, the rough wood ceiling above her seemed very close, the small, irregularly spaced support beams almost near enough to touch. She tried to raise one hand, but her arm was too heavy. What was wrong with her? Maybe she'd had too much wine last night, celebrating her engagement with 'Tavio and Poppy. No, that wasn't last night . . .

The room was perceptibly lighter when she woke again. She remembered the ceiling; it had receded somewhat, and now she had enough presence of mind to wonder what place this was. None of the rooms at Sonrisa looked like this.

Trailing her eyes downward, she noticed the plank wall, the one window dirty and partly boarded up, cutting down on the faint light from outside. *This is very strange*, she thought, but somehow she felt no real curiosity . . .

A beam of sunlight prodded her eyelids open. So it wasn't a dream.

The surface beneath her was very hard. She moved her hand and felt it. A plank of some kind—a table? Turning on her side, she managed to lever herself into a sitting position, letting her legs dangle. From the waist down she was covered with a filthy blanket, obviously someone's clumsy attempt to make her comfortable.

She reached into her memory, looking for answers, but the effort made her head pound. Pressing her hands to her temples, she could actually feel the pulse. For a few seconds the pain increased, until she could sit upright no longer, then she swung her legs up and lay back.

God, what was happening to her? Where was she and why? The flesh on her arms grew tight with goose bumps, and she hugged herself, then tried to rub the chilliness away. She winced when her palm touched the inside of her right forearm, and she raised it to the light. An ugly bruise stood out against the paleness of her skin. An injection—someone had given her an injection . . .

Then she remembered. She had been at an airport, going on a trip with . . . with Donovan. He had touched her, kissed her. "I have a lot to tell you," he'd said. There was a helicopter, not the one he'd flown in Mexico. This one was different, dark and shiny, sleek looking. They were going away in the helicopter, she and Donovan.

The memory completed itself and she moaned. Dead! He was dead, shot and left to lie in the darkness, and she wanted him to get up, but the man said Donovan wouldn't be coming with them . . .

Santos. León Santos. He had killed Donovan and drugged her.

She knew she should feel something, react somehow, but the knowledge was too enormous to comprehend. Her mind simply turned the facts away, pushed them into some far recess where they would remain, impotent, unable to hurt her.

The tabletop grew harder as she lay there, rubbing against her spine. Responding to the stimulus, she sat up again, this time sliding forward until her feet reached the floor. For a moment the room swam and her vision dimmed, but she resolutely fought down the weakness and remained on her feet.

When she was sure the dizziness had passed, she began a methodical exploration of her prison. Other than the table, there was no furniture, only a number of wooden crates piled in two of the corners. They looked like boxes canned goods were packed in, but the painted lettering on the thin slats was too faded to read. She also found a burlap bag half full of assorted clothing. It looked as if it might be verminous, and she dropped the sack without touching anything in it.

There was only one door, and, unlike the rest of the structure, it appeared to be heavy and solid. The knob was rusty, but it didn't rattle when she tried it. Locked from outside, she decided, but not with a key. Probably braced with a board, or maybe padlocked.

The single window was small, but she could have wiggled through it had it not been for the board nailed across it. For several minutes she yanked and pulled, until one of her fingernails ripped down into the quick. A drop of blood welled up, and she watched with detachment as it slowly rolled to the tip of her finger and dropped off.

Standing on tiptoe, her head barely cleared the lower sill. The wooden crates looked sturdy enough, so she turned one upside down and stood on it.

The view was desolate. This place, whatever it was, appeared to be isolated in the mountains. The terrain was rugged, all crags and hard, cracked earth with no vegetation to relieve its harshness. The roof's wide overhang blocked out the sun, but it beat down fiercely on the high peaks to the east. There was no sign of a road or a trail, no other human being, to reassure her that she wasn't alone.

Not fair, it's not fair . . .

"This isn't fair!" she screamed. "Why am I being punished? I haven't done anything!"

She beat on the window, smashing one of the two remaining panes. "I won't stay here, I won't! Do you hear me? I won't stay!"

The crate tipped and she slid off, scraping her ankle. With a strength born of fury too long suppressed, she grabbed the crate and hurled it across the room. It didn't break, so she followed it, kicked it, threw it again and again and again. When it lay in scattered splinters, she attacked another of the boxes and began the ritual anew.

"I won't stay here, I won't! I won't! *I won't stay here!*"

A sound at the door sent her scurrying into the corner. She raised a broken slat and backed into a crouch.

When the door opened, she tensed, ready to spring.

"That won't do you no good, lady." A stocky man, the one who had attacked her at Wynette's, stepped into the room, blocking the exit. He held a gun in his hand. "Now, put it down and come on over here."

She shook her head mutely.

"Have it your way. I just came in to tell you to save your breath. No way you can get outta here." He backed out the door. "You settle down and you'll get something to eat. Keep it up and I'll let you starve."

The door closed and she was alone again. But she crouched in the corner a long time, still holding her pitiful weapon.

By ten o'clock that morning, Wynette was dancing with impatience, driving Felix to the brink of a rude remark concerning childish behavior. "Why haven't they called? Don't they know how worried we are?" She stopped her pacing long enough to flop down in the rattan chair but immediately jumped to her feet again. "We should've heard somethin' from 'Tavio by now. I'm gettin' worried."

Felix caught her left hand as she passed and tugged her down next to him on the love seat. "Would you calm down? The note said he'd call when they got to the island, so he will. Maybe things just aren't settled yet."

"Felix, he left sometime before we called from Atascadero. So he's been gone at least eighteen hours, maybe more." Close to tears and physically worn down from the long drive the night before, Wynette was in no mood to be placated. "I think somethin' bad has happened."

"Come on, Wyn, don't look for trouble. Even in the

Sikorsky, it's seven hours from here to Santa Marta, and we don't know where he had to go to pick her up." He hoped he sounded convincing, but the truth was that he too was getting edgy. "Hell, they might still be in the air."

Wyn sighed. "Yeah, I guess so. That Mitch guy said he overheard the truck driver say somethin' about Klamath Falls. Think she might've got all the way to Oregon?"

"Beats me. Any farther north than Santa Monica and I'm lost." He stood up and pulled her to her feet. "I'll make you a deal. If we haven't heard anything by the time we cook breakfast, eat it and clean up the mess, we'll call Herrera."

Wynette readily agreed, glad for any excuse to put her twitchy hands to work, and the two of them happily bumped into each other on their respective paths between cabinets, refrigerator, and stove.

As it turned out, the first batch of hotcakes weren't off the griddle when the phone rang.

"Now, did I call it, or did I call it?" Felix gloated as he trotted off to answer it, Wynette almost literally at his heels.

But after he said hello, his end of the conversation consisted exclusively of monosyllables. "Yeah . . . when? . . . right . . . where?" From the way his face had rearranged itself, Wynette knew it wasn't the call they'd been expecting.

He replaced the receiver and looked at the floor; Wynette went cold inside. "That was the Salinas hospital," he said. "Jay was admitted last night. He was shot. He's okay, awake and everything. He told them to call us."

Wynette had listened intently to what he didn't say. "And Anna? What about Anna?" She clutched his arm in a frenzy of fear.

He shook his head. "I don't know. He was alone."

Wynette fell into his arms and began to cry.

"Lucky for you, you've got a hard head." Felix's hearty words sounded forced, and his handsome face showed the strain he'd been under.

Donovan eyed his partner from the hospital bed where he was uncomfortably propped with too many pillows behind his back. "Lucky for me Santos is a lousy shot." He plucked at the bandage decorating the crown of his head. The adhesive made a complete circle, almost touching his eyebrows. "This damn thing itches. All it needed was some iodine and a Band-Aid. Hand me my clothes, will you."

Felix opened the tiny closet doors, removed the clothing and tossed it to Donovan. "Don't you think you should wait to be discharged?"

"Wait? I feel like I've been waiting forever." He jerked the hospital gown loose, ripping the back ties. "We're getting out of here now. Where's Wynette?"

"Downstairs trying to get you sprung. Maybe we ought to look into an accident policy." Felix watched his friend pull on his pants, one slow leg at a time, then handed him the shirt, trying not to pay any attention to the bloodstains on it. "Seems like you've developed a talent for coming out on the short end."

"What I've developed is terminal stupidity." He didn't ignore the stains as Felix had; he looked at them long and hard before putting on the shirt. "I walked right into it last night, Felix. If I hadn't been so damned sure of myself, if I'd checked out the area, it wouldn't have happened." He swayed suddenly and caught at the bed for support.

Felix offered a helping hand, which Donovan ignored. "You're not ready for this, *amigo*. You should be in that bed, not holding on to it."

Donovan refused his assistance. "What else did Herrera say?"

"Just that he had a lead, one of the geologists who worked up the report on the mine. Herrera tracked him down, explained the facts of life, and the guy spilled his guts. Didn't have any idea all the workers at the mine were illegals, or so he claims. He's probably just allergic to the word *accessory*."

The door opened silently and Wynette stuck her head

around, then followed it with the rest of her. Ashen of face, she took in the bandages first, then the bloodstains. "Oh, my God," she whispered.

Felix quickly closed the short distance between them and took both her upper arms in his hands. "If you start that again, so help me . . ."

"It's not nearly as bad as it looks, Wyn," Donovan reassured her. "See? I walk and talk and all that good stuff." He slipped his bare feet into the shoes Felix had tossed to him along with the clothes; the way his head felt, he didn't think he could manage bending over to fool with his socks. "Do I need to sign anything before we leave?"

"No, I paid cash, so it's all clear." Wynette cleared her throat to get rid of the teary lump that roughened her voice. "Jay, are you sure you're up to this?"

"Yeah." His eyes turned dark with renewed anger. "I've never felt better. Come on, we're going to Mexico."

Anna sat cross-legged in the center of the table in the center of the room. Since the rat had darted from one corner to disappear into the burlap bag of clothing, she'd been careful not to even let her feet dangle. If she had to fight rats on top of everything else . . .

She still hadn't cried for Donovan, and the lack of appropriate response bothered her. *But it wouldn't be for him*, she reasoned. *He's out of it. It would be for me, for what I've missed . . . for what I'll never know. So why can't I cry for me?* She didn't know the answer but suspected it was because she was past caring, past feeling. In a way, she was grateful for the numbness; it seemed that she'd been in emotional pain for so long she'd almost forgotten what it was not to hurt.

The light in the room had been dim for some time now. She had watched the sun creep up past the window, and as soon as its rays disappeared from her view, the light began to fade, blocked by the deep overhang of the roof. It could have been midafternoon or dusk—she couldn't tell. It didn't matter anyway. There was nothing to see except cobwebs, dust, and the accumulated trash of unknown years.

She licked her lips and winced when her tongue traced the dry, cracked surfaces. How long had it been since she'd had a drink of water? she wondered. At least twelve or fourteen hours. The drug she'd been given had aggravated the dehydration process. The inside of her mouth felt cottony, with an unhealthy taste. Maybe soon someone would bring water and food, though she could truthfully say she had no interest in eating.

For a long time she concentrated on not concentrating, on filling her mind with meaningless bits of trivia—the names of her favorite movies, books she had loved, and books she had hated—anything to keep all the terrifying thoughts at bay. Otherwise she would be lost to despair, sunk in a limbo of hopelessness and fear that she didn't have the strength to face.

Gradually, though, the numbness began to wear off, like an anesthetic after dental work. The feeling began to return in slow stages, sneaking up on her so quietly she was hardly aware of what was happening. First she thought of her grandfather. Throughout the years she had stored up enough happy memories to fill a dozen scrapbooks, and one by one she began to take them out and examine them: the puppy he'd given her for Christmas one year when she wasn't much bigger than the dog—she had named it Rudolph by some convoluted reasoning that had made perfect sense, but only to her; the first time he'd let her steer the launch—oh, she'd felt so powerful, controlling that huge piece of floating wood and metal all by her nine-year-old self; the year he'd let her redecorate the house, leaving all the planning, choosing, and arranging solely to her discretion—she'd been fifteen then, with absolute faith in her sophisticated tastes. Two years later, she'd looked at the gaudy mess she'd made and promptly had it all redone, loving him even more for never having told her how much he must have hated seeing those lovely rooms buried in abstract prints and shag carpeting.

Now he was gone, forever and irrevocably, leaving her rootless.

'Tavio was gone too, just as irrevocably. Funny, she'd always thought only death could be final, had never considered the possibility of losing someone in life. What right had 'Tavio to even be alive, when he meant nothing of importance to anyone, had nothing of value to offer? Not like Poppy . . . and Donovan.

There it was, the one fact she'd tried to deny, the one loss she couldn't bear to face. *This is the way it would feel*, she thought, *if half my soul were suddenly torn away*. An endless black void waiting to swallow her . . .

"I refuse," she said aloud. Then she curled up on her side, knees drawn tightly against her stomach, and plunged herself into sleep.

An undefined noise disturbed her and she shifted slightly, trying to settle her hip into a more comfortable position, but the surface beneath her was hard and unyielding, pressing against her painfully. She was sore from shoulder to knee, but, still mostly asleep, she registered only the fact and not the cause of it. She stirred again and murmured. The sound of her own voice roused her more fully, and she opened her eyes.

Before her stood a shadowy figure, illumined by a single flickering source of light. From her prone position, she saw the figure askance. It seemed to waver and tilt, then it moved closer.

Completely awake now, she gasped and sat up so quickly her head swam. She opened her mouth to scream, thinking she was caught in some terrible waking nightmare.

Then the figure spoke. "*Señorita?*"

She simply stared for a moment, unable to reconcile the soft, almost servile voice with the apparition that flickered eerily in front of her. As her mind cleared, so did the scene, and the figure resolved itself into a short, thin Mexican of indeterminate years. He was smeared with dirt, his clothes filthy. He held a lantern in one hand, a tin plate in the other, and his broad, brown face was a study in perplexity. "*Señorita?*" he repeated hesitantly.

She pulled her knees against her chest, wrapped her arms around them. "What do you want?" In spite of her fear, her voice was firm, and she was proud of at least that small victory. *If he touches me*, she thought, *I'll claw his eyes out.*

But he made no move other than to extend the plate and smile tentatively. "*Aquí esta su comida, señorita.*"

She continued to look at him steadily. "Just put it down and get out."

"Ah, *Norteamericana*," he said, as if that lone fact explained the oddness of the situation in which he found himself. "So I speak English." He gestured again with the plate. "Eat, *señorita*, please. No more except tomorrow."

"Until tomorrow," she corrected automatically. When she realized what she'd done, she nearly laughed aloud at the irony. This man was her jailer and she was giving him English lessons!

He seemed to find nothing inappropriate in her response. "*Sí,*" he beamed, "until tomorrow. *Grácias, señorita.* I must speak good English for Texas."

His accent was so heavy Anna had to strain to understand him, and for a moment she was tempted to speak in his own language and lessen the barrier between them. Then she reconsidered. It could work to her advantage to be thought ignorant; people tended to speak more freely when they felt they weren't being overheard. Besides, his face was eager and friendly, nonthreatening. It probably wouldn't take much to turn him into an ally.

"Texas?" she encouraged, taking the plate from him. It was covered with something gloppy—canned pork and beans, she thought, not really interested.

"*Sí,* San Antonio. My brother, he live there." Once

started, the words poured out of his mouth like water from an uncorked bottle.

His name, she learned, was Jesús, and his brother had promised to help him find work in the mecca of San Antonio. His exact travel plans were rather vague, and Anna knew he was planning to cross the border illegally. About everything else, he was overwhelmingly precise. His sisters and brothers, all eleven of them, were fine people, his wife the best cook, his children the most beautiful. He himself was the hardest worker Mexico had ever produced, and the new life he would make for his family would be the envy of every man in his village . . .

If he noticed that she merely pushed the revolting beans around on the plate without tasting them, he couldn't find time during his monologue to comment on the fact. Anna let him rattle on, listening with only a portion of her mind. He seemed to be a good man; she felt not a touch of anxiety about his presence. If she could win his loyalty, or at least figure out how to manipulate him, she just might be able to escape from this place. Wherever this place was, she reminded herself. The first order of business was to look around, find out what obstacles she would face.

"Jesús," she interrupted, "am I allowed to leave this building?"

"*Qué?*"

"I mean, there's no bathroom in here." She tried to look distressed, which wasn't all that difficult. The pressure in her bladder had been steadily building into actual discomfort for some time.

He shook his head, obviously confused. "Tell me, *señorita*, I help you."

She sighed. "A latrine, Jesús, a toilet, a bathroom . . ."

"Ah!" He brightened. "*Sí*, I forget; *mi jefe*, he tell me this thing. *Vámos.*"

Taking her arm almost reverently, he helped her from the table, escorted her to the door.

It was dark outside, that thick, complete blackness never

seen in the cities. Jesús held the lantern high, but the light it cast was feeble against the mountain night. Still, Anna couldn't help the thrill that ran through her, heightening her senses. She was outside, free, even if only for a minute or two. The air was chill, with a bite that promised uncomfortably cold temperatures before daylight, but Anna didn't mind. The gooseflesh on her arms made her feel more alive.

The toilet facilities lay fifty yards or so from the tiny structure where Anna had been held, in a straight line from the door. There were at least two other buildings along the path, both of them inhabited. Anna sensed rather than saw them, but she could hear the subdued murmur of voices as she passed.

With new hope and determination, she looked up at the stars—bright, distant points that shimmered in the velvet sky. *I gave up too soon*, she thought, *way too soon. Wherever I am, there's a way out and I'll find it. I swear I will.*

"I think we would be foolish not to take more men with us," Herrera said. "Santos would not leave such a place unguarded."

"More men make more noise," Donovan responded. "The three of us are enough." He leaned back against the chair, trying to ease muscles drawn tight with tension and fatigue. It was late, and they'd been going at it for hours, reviewing all that Herrera had learned, considering options, making and remaking plans. His head hurt, but he stubbornly refuted the pain, pushing it away with the force of his obsessive anger. During the times when the throbbing became too severe to ignore, he used it as fuel, energy to keep him alert.

For a moment, no one said anything. Donovan's temper had escaped his formidable control several times already during the evening, and neither Herrera nor Felix was anxious for a repeat performance. Wynette, who had made the trip in spite of Donovan's strong protests, had already gone up to bed, her nerves too frazzled to withstand any more of his biting sarcasm.

Then Felix broke the silence. "Jay," he said gently, "what if she's not there?"

"Why would she not be there?" Herrera said. "The mine is remote and well protected, and Santos has no idea we know about it . . ."

Felix nodded. "I understand that, but . . ."

"He means she may be dead." Donovan spoke flatly, betraying none of the violent emotion that had been choking him since he woke up in a hospital bed. Felix had finally put into words what all of them feared, the one possibility Donovan skirted both mentally and verbally.

A muscle twitched in Herrera's jaw. "A thought we have all had to deal with. But it is unlikely at this point."

"According to the 'godfather'?" Felix sneered. "That's the craziest thing of all. You go to see him on a hunch, and he tells you everything you want to know? I wouldn't trust him as far as I could throw him with one hand."

Herrera smiled grimly. "It was more than a 'hunch', my friend. Santos is a small shell on a large beach; he had to have backing to get this far in his schemes. *El Patrón* was the logical choice, since I knew Santos had met him through Don Roberto. As for the rest," he shrugged, "I suppose it would seem strange to you. But *El Patrón* is a sensible man, and once he understood that the case against Santos, and ultimately against him, could be made without Anna's testimony, he saw the matter in a different light. He has nothing to fear from lawyers and courtrooms, of course; he is far too powerful. But if he became a party to Anna's murder under these circumstances, he would lose the respect of his associates. Anna is also powerful, through her grandfather's many alliances; *El Patrón* realizes this even if she doesn't. Now he only wants Santos, almost as badly as we do, to save face and protect his reputation as a fair man."

"We've been all through this," Donovan broke in, pushing to his feet, "and it all comes down to the same bottom line. She's in a mining camp in the mountains, waiting for Santos to put a bullet through her head. We're going in after her. We leave at first light, and there's still a lot to do, so let's get to it."

"Not yet." Herrera too rose to his feet. He was several inches shorter than Donovan, slimly built, yet his presence was imposing. "There is still a matter for us to discuss."

"Anna." Donovan had been expecting it.

"As you say. Anna. She is very important to me, Donovan; she is family. More to the point, she was entrusted to my care by a man I loved and respected more than any other. I intend to honor my commitment."

"She won't marry you." Though he'd come to admire Herrera and think of him almost as a friend, Donovan felt himself on the edge of violence at that moment.

"Perhaps not. She is an independent woman, and she will make her own decisions. But be warned, Donovan. If she chooses me, you will not see her again. And if she chooses you, I will do everything in my power to change her mind."

The men faced each other down, like two wolves trying to claim the same territory. "She won't choose you," Donovan said finally, "and you won't change her mind. She belongs with me."

Herrera considered his words for a moment, then he nodded. "We will see, my friend."

The thing was said, out in the open, and now it was put aside. The three of them fell to working out details, gathering and packing the necessary desert survival gear, rehearsing every step of their plan over and over again until each of them could recite it in his sleep.

But like a rank odor, one thought hovered in the room, intrusive and insidious: what if they were too late?

Jesús made his appearance shortly after sunrise, bringing with him another plate of beans and a chipped mug half filled with hot, strong coffee.

"*Buenos días*," he greeted her. "I bring you . . . *desayuno?*"

"Breakfast," she supplied, flexing her knee to work out the stiffness. Jesús had thoughtfully provided her with a blanket the night before, but she had stubbornly refused to share the floor with the rats, so she'd remained curled up on top of the table. "Thank you, Jesús, but I'm really not very hungry right now."

"But you must eat, *señorita*." His concern showed in a puckered frown. "I get special, only for you. We do not eat yet."

Though he had spoken matter-of-factly, with no thought of making himself sound pitiable, Anna couldn't help but feel sad and more than a little angry. The little man's garrulity had provided her with many facts, and she now knew that he was one of a group who were waiting to be transported to the States. Part of their payment for this service was made in hard labor, working to clear rubble in the mine that apparently lay nearby, making room for the "other men" to work. Their days were long, from sunup to sundown, and they ate only twice a day. Jesús told her his group had been there nearly two weeks, and now *el jefe* was preparing to move them out the next day.

"No, really, I don't want anything. You eat it, Jesús; you need food to work."

He made one more token protest, then began to shovel the food in. Occasionally he would glance at her as though reaffirming her permission. In less than three minutes, the plate was empty.

"Ah, *grácias, mi carita señorita*. Now I go."

"Wait." During the night, Anna had decided not to try to enlist Jesús's help in trying to escape; she liked him too much to put him in such a dangerous position. But she had to make the attempt herself, and there was no point in putting it off. "Before you leave, I'd like to go to the latrine again."

"*Naturalamente.*" He grinned at her, showing a wide gap where he'd lost at least one tooth. "I take you. *El jefe*, he say to see you are okay."

In the early morning light, Anna got her first real look at her surroundings. As she'd thought, there were two buildings at right angles to the small shack where she stayed. The toilet was tacked onto the back of the second building, obviously a recent addition. The wood wasn't as weathered and the door hung straight, a contrast to the dilapidated condition of the other structures. To the left was a larger building with a porch; a battered military-type jeep was parked in front of it. An office of some kind? she wondered. If so, there were probably watchful eyes peering out at her right now. Fortunately, the door to the latrine couldn't be seen by anyone who might be looking out those windows.

A short distance beyond what she assumed were the barracks that housed Jesús and his companions, she could see a group of people walking toward a mine entrance. There weren't more than a dozen, she judged, and none of them appeared to be armed. Probably the laborers, she decided.

Far to the right of that entrance she saw what she thought was a smelter, but she detected no activity there. Common sense told her that unskilled workers couldn't possibly do the actual mining and smelting. Perhaps the experts didn't start their workday until later in the morning. That meant her best chance would be now, before the camp really started operations.

Her eyes moved over the barren, rocky face of the mountain, taking in the spotty clumps of dried vegetation, the sharp, broken boulders that littered the hard earth. Some of the boulders were large enough to provide a hiding place, but most of them were smaller, scattered in increasing quantities closer to the mine entrance.

Then she saw what she'd been looking for. To the left of the main entrance, so far away she'd nearly missed it, was another hole in the face of the mountain. Another mine, she thought, played out and abandoned. None of the laborers even turned in that direction, and she could see no sign that it was being worked. If she could make it that far without being seen, maybe she'd have a chance. Surely no one would think she'd actually hide right under their noses; they'd assume she had headed down the mountain, away from the camp.

Her heartbeat accelerated as her body geared up, sending the adrenalin racing through her veins.

Jesús politely faced away from the latrine as she opened the door. Inside, she leaned weakly against the wall, praying that her nerve wouldn't fail at the last minute.

"Jesús," she called after a short interval, injecting all the alarm she felt into her voice. "Jesús, I'm sick. I need help."

Instantly he knocked on the door. "*Qué? Señorita*, what is wrong?"

She opened the door a crack. It wasn't hard to fake being ill. Her hands trembled, a sheen of perspiration lined her upper lip in spite of the morning chill; she knew her face was pale. "Please get someone to help me, Jesús."

He hopped back and forth in agitation. "*Sí, el jefe*, I will bring *el jefe* . . ."

"No!" she cried in alarm. "It's a woman thing, Jesús. Can you get one of the women to help me?"

"They are all at the mine, *señorita*. You will stay here until I come back?"

"Yes, I'll stay here. I'm too sick to go anywhere. Just hurry, Jesús." She exhaled heavily for emphasis. "Hurry now."

A second after he had turned away, Anna slipped out the door and ran, stumbling time and again on the cracked rocks, the torn earth. She didn't pause until she reached the shelter of the first boulder, then she flattened her body against it, gasping for air. She hadn't considered what effect the thinner atmosphere would have on her laboring lungs.

One breath, two, then she risked a look past the boulder. Jesús hadn't yet reached the mine entrance, but he was moving away from her at a sharp angle, so it was unlikely he would spot her.

She waited only a second more, gathering her strength

for the next sprint. When she stopped again, her goal was less than thirty yards away. It wasn't a mine entrance at all, she saw, but a cave. She hoped it would be large, with plenty of room to lose herself until nightfall, but it really made no difference now. Even if it was nothing more than a hole, it was her only refuge and she was stuck with it.

In the distance she could see Jesús and a woman, both running toward the camp. She would be in their line of vision for another few seconds, then she could make the final dash.

Now! Over the treacherous ground she flew, heedless of the shards of rock that cut through the soles of her shoes. She gained the mouth of the cave and collapsed just inside. The furious pounding of her heart filled her ears, and her chest heaved as she gulped in the air.

Reaction set in, leaving her limp with relief. For a long time she lay still, too weak to move. Down at the camp there was probably a flurry of activity—men shouting, pounding the hard earth in pursuit—but for now she didn't care. She was safely away and that was all that mattered.

She didn't hear the man's approach; the softer dirt in the cave muffled his footsteps. His voice, when it sounded, cut through her frayed nerves like a machete, locking her muscles into place, and she nearly choked on her terror.

"Nice of you to drop by, honey. A man gets lonesome up here all by himself."

She knew that voice and the face that went with it. Fat jowls, mean eyes, and a gun.

First she screamed. Then she fainted.

—13—

THE THREE MEN perched in the rocks high above the camp and surveyed the scene below them with anticipatory satisfaction. The geologist had provided them with an excellent map, accurate and detailed even to the several unmistakable landmarks that had guided them here. They'd had no trouble finding the camp, though it had taken them more than an hour of rough trekking through the dim light of early dawn to reach this place, and it wasn't more than a mile from the helicopter.

Now Donovan stirred restlessly, shifting his weight to his good knee. "Something's going on down there. I don't like it."

In the clearing below, tiny men ran from building to building, sometimes waving their arms. An occasional shout drifted up to the watchers, but the words were always too faint to understand.

"Well, we can't go in until the commotion dies down. Too many weapons and too many trigger fingers." Felix eased back on his haunches, away from the edge of the promontory, before he stood up. "I think your lady made a break for it, Jay. Those birds are definitely looking for something, and they're in one hell of a hurry."

Herrera, who'd been keeping himself well out of the way of his more knowledgeable and experienced companions, looked suddenly eager, with more expression on his face than either Felix or Donovan had ever seen. "Then she could be anywhere, even nearby. If we scouted the area, perhaps we could find her and be gone before those down there"—he jerked his head contemptuously in the direction of the camp—"even realize what has happened."

Donovan shook his head, never taking his eyes from the scene below. "Take a good look at this place, Herrera. Anna's no fool, and she'd know she couldn't make it up here on her own. The face of this wall is nearly straight up, and the look of the country to the south is enough to scare a mountain goat. If she ran, it was in the other direction, down the mountain, not up."

"I agree," Felix said. "And since there's no way to get from here to there without being seen, I think we should stay put, give it a few more minutes and see what happens."

Herrera's excitement subsided as he considered the validity of what his companions had said. "You are right," he pronounced. "I'm afraid my thinking is less clear than it should be."

"You're entitled," Donovan said. God knew his own reaction had been to charge down to the clearing, gun drawn and blazing; if his training and experience hadn't reasserted itself, he'd be down there now, putting all their lives in danger with no reasonable goal as a trade-off. He eased his body around the jagged rocks and found a reasonably smooth surface on which to sit. Shaking a cigarette out of the crumpled pack from the pocket of his field jacket, he lit it and inhaled deeply. "None of us are thinking straight right now. There's too much at stake."

"Just keep it cool, for Anna's sake," Felix reminded them. "We're the only cavalry she's got." He leaned against the largest boulder and snaked his way forward, climbing up until his head cleared the top. "Hey, take a look."

Donovan and Herrera scrambled to the edge again, lying prone. Following the direction of Felix's pointing finger, they could see two figures, too distant to be recognized, approaching the camp from the northwest.

"It's a woman," Donovan said after a moment. As he

watched, he could barely discern her long hair whipping away from her head, glinting gold in the early sunlight. "It's her. But I can't tell who's with her."

"Crewe." Herrera's eyes were narrowed, giving his face the lean, hungry look of a feral animal. "He trots like a pig."

"She doesn't look like she's hurt. At least she's walking under her own power." Felix's assessment, being less emotional and more practical, was also more valuable. If she were injured, they could have real problems carrying her out over this terrain. "Where's he taking her?"

"The small building, probably the dynamite shack." Donovan rolled over onto his back, pulled a gun out of his belt, checked the cartridge. "We start working our way down now. By the time we get there, everything will have smoothed out. The shack's closest to us from the southern approach, but unless there's a back door, we'll be exposed when we go in."

"No problem," Felix said. "I'll take the west corner, Herrera the east, you go in like blockbusters."

"Right. No problem." Donovan smiled at his friend, remembering the phrase's many applications in the past. It had been used to describe everything from getting a date to getting the Cong. Since both of them were still around, he had to assume the words had at least some validity.

"Okay, let's move."

Donovan took the lead, and they started the tedious descent, single file through narrow gaps between the towering red rocks, sliding more often than they walked. There was, of course, no trail other than what they could forge for themselves.

Coming back this way would be even more difficult because of the sharp incline, but the formations, tight and nearly impassable, would also be their best means of self-defense. A decent head start would give them all the advantage they would need, for they had already noted the bad turns, the loose rocks, the ledges. While they were making time, their pursuers would be scrabbling for hand-holds.

We're going to do it this time, Donovan thought, mechanically placing one foot in front of the other, his eyes darting restlessly. *We're really going to do it. Hang on, baby, we're almost there.*

Anna held a shaking hand to her bruised face, holding back the tears. She knew she was lucky to have gotten off so lightly; no one in the camp, not even Jesús, would have raised a hand to help her if she were being beaten to death.

Now she was back in the hovel, thrown through the door like a sack of garbage. When she heard the brace slide into place, she knew it signalled the end of the few amenities she'd enjoyed up until now. Real luxuries, like an occasional drink of water.

Wearily she boosted herself back up on her tabletop perch, noticing for the first time the deep scratch marks in the surface of the wood. Maybe she could pass the time writing her autobiography, carving it out for posterity. She could call it "Reflections in a Mining Camp."

"Oh, God," she groaned. "What's wrong with me?" *Stupid question*, she answered herself. How is one supposed to behave when one is waiting to be killed? Scratching her life story into a piece of wood made just as much sense as crying—both were utterly pointless.

She drew her knees up into their familiar position, pointing her face toward the window. There wasn't much action and no plot to speak of, but it was better than watching the dust settle. If she could only clear her mind, perhaps she could come up with something, another plan. Like the window. The night before, her perspective had been different. The window had appeared to be useless as a possible escape route. But now she looked at it more closely. True, it was small, but so was she. It was possible that she could wriggle through it; the trick would be to pull off the board and break out the rest of the panes without making any noise. Maybe they were loose and would just pull out . . .

Her eyes probed the ancient wooden frame, looking for signs of rot or weakness, then swept past the interior of the shack to the mountains beyond. A great outcropping of rock, scattered down from a higher ridge to the edge of the clearing like giant, misshapen marbles, seemed much nearer than it had the day before. She should have run that way. She might have broken her neck, but she'd have felt much less a fool.

A movement, furtive and fleeting, arrested her attention. She watched carefully, and in a few moments she saw it again. It wasn't an animal, not moving like that!

Excitement filled her, and she jumped from the table in her haste to reach the window. From the top of a crate, she pressed her face against the dirty panes, starving for the food of hope.

A man! No, *three* men, all moving with the stealth and patience of cat burglars. Which meant they didn't want to be seen by anyone in the camp. In spite of her mental warning, she toyed with the idea that they'd come to rescue her. *Stupid*, she told herself. *No one knows you're here; probably no one cares* . . .

Something about the man in the lead touched a chord of memory. Even if his face hadn't been shaded by a cap, he was too far away for her to see his features.

Donovan had walked like that, she recalled suddenly, with a springy motion, as though he were a tightly wound coil. Everything about him, in fact, had been suffused with an energy barely held in check. It was one of the things about him that had taken her breath away. And now he was gone, as dead as she would be soon . . .

"No," she breathed, watching the man turn to speak to one of his companions, "it can't be . . ."

She held her breath, not daring to project her fantasies past the room where she stood trapped. But as he drew nearer and nearer, the fantasy broke free of the bonds of limited imagination and became reality. It was him! Jay! "Jay, Jay, Jay," she whispered frantically, tears streaming down her cheeks. And 'Tavio was with him.

Mesmerized with wonder, she watched them approach, unable to react.

Donovan saw her face at the window. Raising one finger to his lips, he gestured to her to remain silent and, in the same movement, waved Felix and Herrera forward to take their places.

At the back corner of the building, he paused to check his surroundings. The dynamite shack seemed to be unguarded, but he'd learned the hard way never to trust appearances. Looking to Felix and Herrera for corroboration, Donovan accepted their assurances that all was quiet; keeping his back against the wall, he began working his way to the locked door.

They weren't overly concerned with security, he noted gratefully, tugging at the heavy bar that rested sideways across the door, held at each end by a U-shaped piece of metal bolted to the door frame. Crewe apparently felt confident that no one at the camp would take the risk of trying to help her. The bar resisted for a moment; one of the U's had been dented, perhaps by a well-aimed bootheel. Then it was free, and he tossed it to Felix.

Anna nearly fell out the door, throwing her arms around him, saying his name over and over like a chant. He hushed her with a brief kiss, lifting her off her feet to carry her behind the shack, out of sight.

Herrera's hoarse shout brought them up short. "Donovan!"

Spinning Anna out of the way, Donovan dropped into a crouch, the automatic extended toward the four men running at them across the compound. Three of the attackers held crude weapons, boards and chains; the fourth carried a rifle.

He propelled her behind the shack with a brutal shove.

"Go for the rocks," he yelled, "we're right behind you!" He heard her running footsteps, and part of his mind noted that they sounded strong and even. The rest of his attention was focused on holding the four men at bay until she was well away from the danger. "You next, Herrera, get behind her!"

As Herrera darted past, Donovan and Felix closed ranks.

"Hold it!" Felix shouted at the advancing men, who by now were less than twenty yards away and still coming. They ignored the command, and the one with the rifle aimed his weapon.

Without taking the time to worry about his action, Donovan fired off two rounds. The first shell struck short, kicking up a tiny plume of red dust. The second one struck its target, and the man dropped his rifle, his left arm suddenly useless.

Left without an armed leader, the wounded man's cohorts stopped their headlong rush, looking uncertainly at one another, clearly unwilling to risk being shot themselves.

Felix took advantage of their confusion, fired another round near their feet for emphasis, then he and Donovan fled the camp, their boots pounding against the unyielding earth as loudly as their hearts pounded against their ribs. Far behind them, voices were raised in frantic protest, and the sound of an engine starting up carried across the human noise.

"Should've disabled the jeep," Donovan panted.

"Now you tell me."

They overtook Herrera and Anna at the base of the rockfall, then the four of them plunged into a narrow crevice nearly hidden by great, jagged boulders.

Climbing steadily and rapidly in single file, the weary group wasted neither time nor breath in talking. Only their labored breathing and the crunch of soles on rock disturbed the stillness of the morning. Even the hue and cry from the camp had receded, finally fading altogether.

With Felix leading the way, Anna was sandwiched safely between 'Tavio in front and Jay, who constantly kept one hand against her back, as much for his own assurance as hers, she guessed. Her mind whirled with questions and conjecture, but she followed the men's lead and threw all of her efforts into the grueling climb. She knew there would be time for answers later.

Once she lost her footing and fell several feet, scraping her palm as she grabbed for a handhold, then Donovan was there. He braced her body with his, steadied her, urged her forward again while 'Tavio reached for her hand to pull her forward. Soon the rhythm of survival reasserted itself, and she forgot the rawness of her palms, the burning in her lungs. There was only the instant: feet moving mechanically, bleeding hands feeling for a grip, eyes that saw nothing but the next step. Time had no meaning, the sun inching its way high overhead had no purpose but to bring sweat to the surface of your skin. Effort became existence.

Donovan's hand on her arm halted her movement. "You can stop now, duchess," he said softly. "We're here."

She blinked and looked around. They were standing on a small area of level ground, and not more than thirty feet away was a lovely black machine to fly them away from this place. The men were watching her—Felix with a proud smile, 'Tavio with a sad expression she couldn't quite comprehend.

Donovan's arms went around her as she sagged. "Just a little farther, then you can rest."

She looked at his face, seeing him for the first time. The skin under his eyes was dark, almost purple, and the hollows in his cheeks threw his bones into sharp relief. He'd removed his cap, exposing the startlingly white bandage, now stained with red.

She gasped. "Jay, you're bleeding."

"It'll stop." He nodded toward the helicopter. "Come on, we're not out of the woods yet."

Felix took the controls, while the others settled in the passenger seats. Anna thought the whirring of the motors was the most beautiful sound she'd ever heard. Sighing, she closed her eyes, loving the sway of the helicopter as it rose into the air, then hung suspended for an instant when Felix turned it toward the south.

Donovan waited until Anna seemed relaxed, then he eased into the co-pilot's seat and slipped the headset over his ears, motioning Felix to do the same.

"Easier going out than coming in," Felix said. "Maybe because I can see."

Donovan chuckled. "With the instruments in here, you don't need eyes." He surveyed the area critically. From the air, the red-brown land looked like a scene from Dante. Some of the ravines were so narrow and deep the sun didn't reach their bottoms, and the cruel peaks and crags seemed to be ripped from the earth. A cruel and deadly place, he thought. "I don't get it," he said aloud. "How do they move stuff in and out?"

"Same way we did," Felix answered. "Or maybe they use that." As they topped a peak and dropped into a canyon, he pointed down to a narrow, crooked ribbon of track that had just come into view.

"A mountain goat couldn't use that," Donovan said.

"Hate to make a liar out of you, buddy. Take a look."

Out of a sheer rock wall, it seemed, the jeep from the camp made an abrupt appearance. Donovan registered its existence a split second before the first shell exploded off their port side.

"What the hell have they got down there?" Felix yelled, manipulating the controls to gain altitude.

"Looks like a rocket launcher and at least one machine gun. Christ, they must have cleaned out the black market." Another shell exploded. "Get us out of here!"

Too busy with the controls to reply, Felix took them up

sharply, swinging the Sikorsky dangerously near the canyon wall before they cleared it and left the occupants of the jeep to waste their ammo on empty airspace.

A glance over his shoulder told Donovan that Anna was all right, though Herrera seemed to have his hands full keeping her safely seated.

"Next time we want a closer look, let's not take it. I'm not that curious."

Felix didn't seem to find the remark amusing. "We're going to get a real close look at the ground pretty soon." He tapped one of the indicators on the console. "We're losing hydraulic pressure. Sombody got lucky and hit a line."

"How far can we make it?"

"Another two or three miles, then I'll have to set her down."

"That puts us on the edge of the desert." Donovan wished his head would quit hurting; he needed to think, but the damned throbbing interfered.

"Yeah. We didn't plan it so good this time."

Donovan looked back at Anna. She was talking to Herrera, leaning toward him with her hand on his shoulder. She shook her head sharply and tried to rise from her seat, but he grasped her wrist.

Watching the brief byplay, Donovan felt his temper rise. Herrera hadn't wasted any time, he thought bitterly. Already he'd started his campaign.

Then he took a close look at Herrera's face. His normally dark skin seemed unnaturally pale, and a bead of perspiration dotted his high forehead. Something was wrong.

As if she sensed his regard, Anna looked up. With a small, unnoticeable gesture, she managed to convey the information Donovan had been dreading.

"The plan just got worse," he said, facing forward again. "Herrera's been wounded."

—14—

THE SIKORSKY HAD barely cleared the foothills before Felix had to set it down. Now he and Donovan stood outside, staring morosely at the vast expanse of nothing that stretched to the horizon. The only break in the flatness was to the west, where a small mountain range rose from the remnants of the larger one to the north.

The sun, now almost directly overhead, beat down upon the sparse clumps of withered vegetation and dried earth with relentless authority. Man is not in control of this country and never would be, it seemed to say, so don't try to force your puny selves upon me.

"I don't like it," Donovan said. "Do you know the chances against us being able to walk out of here?"

"Better than your chances of finding a taxi. Come on, Jay, you know we're right. Protect Anna and get help for Herrera—that's priority."

"Damn it, don't you think I know that? There are just too many mistakes we could make. The only one of us who knows this country is Herrera, and he can't walk."

"He's already told you what you need to know. It's not really that far; you've got food and plenty of water. It's a straight shot across the plains, and Herrera says you're bound to run into someone once you reach those foothills."

"That's farfetched and you know it. We'd do better to stay put. Tanner knows what we're doing. When we don't show up, he'll come after us."

"Come after us, yeah. But that's no guarantee he'll find us."

"Okay, say we make it," Donovan conceded. "Where does that leave you and Herrera if one of Santos's men spots the chopper and comes to investigate?"

"Right where we'd be regardless of where you are." Stooping, he picked up a stone, hurled it with considerable force into the desert. "Look, Jay, there's no one perfect solution, but this way we're covering more of the bases."

Donovan rubbed his forehead. "Damn, I can't think straight . . ."

"Yeah, a head wound and a week without sleep tends to do that. So listen to me for a change. Herrera and I know the risks, and we've made our decision. Just get Anna out of here. That's what this whole thing is about, right?"

Donovan heard a footfall, turned to watch Anna approach them from the Sikorsky. "How is he?"

She leaned against him gratefully. "Well, the wound's clean, but he's lost a lot of blood and he's very weak. He needs to be in a hospital; if that leg becomes infected, he could lose it."

Neither of the men answered her. They had already faced that possibility and it sickened them both. Octavio Herrera had earned their respect and their friendship; he deserved better than to wind up a cripple.

"He told me what you've all been so secretive about," she continued. "We've got to do it, Jay. If we stay, nobody has a chance." She blinked rapidly, trying not to give in to her weakness. " 'Tavio thinks he and Felix can make a stand here, if it comes to that. And it's only about twenty miles— we can be back with help by tomorrow night."

Looking at her weary face, so full of faith and good intentions, Donovan felt his heart turn over. She'd been through so much, and now she was willing to take this final risk. He didn't think she had any real notion of how dangerous such a trek could be; he was also sure that if she did know, her decision would be the same.

"Okay, duchess. Let's saddle up." He kissed her lightly, then she turned and walked back to the helicopter.

"She's a good person, *amigo*, the best," Felix said when she was out of earshot. "But then, you always did have all the luck."

The suggestion of flatness had been deceptive, an illusion produced by the relative height of the mountains. Actually the land sloped, tapering gradually to the true desert, which was still many miles distant. Occasionally there would be a sharp dip, hidden by a line of elephant trees.

In one such dip Donovan and Anna rested. The trees offered scant shade from the afternoon sun in spite of their thick trunks. Twisted and small-leaved, they grew low to the ground and out, as if the weight of the heat were a tangible thing, pushing on them from above, forcing them to spread as they grew. There was a bit of grass here, but it appeared seldom and then only in solitary wisps, sere and faded.

Donovan passed Anna the canteen and watched her drink. It amazed him that her slender body possessed such reserves of strength; throughout the long afternoon, she'd kept pace with him, never asking to stop, never giving in to the bone-wracking weariness he knew she must be feeling. Again he wondered at the miracle of finding her. Accident or design? What thread of destiny connected them, that a chance encounter on a tiny island had altered their lives so drastically?

She capped the canteen, handed it to him. "Do you know what I'm going to do first when I get home? Take a bath, the longest bath in history. And when I'm finished, I'll take another one." She leaned back on her elbows. "You wouldn't know it to look at me now, but I clean up nicely."

"You mean under all that dirt is a diamond?"

She laughed. "Maybe not a diamond, but at least a zircon." Suddenly serious, she looked at him. "Jay, do you realize you've never seen me under normal conditions?"

"Depends on what you consider normal," he teased. "I don't have any problem with skinny blondes who throw me across hotel rooms. It happens all the time."

Amazingly, she blushed. "That was an accident. I was afraid of you and I overreacted."

He reached for her then, cradling her in his arms, content just to feel her slight weight against him. For a long time they sat that way, not speaking, until she stirred and kissed his chin.

"Yeah, I know," he said. "We've got to move." He released her to drink his own ration from the canteen. "The quicker we get there, the quicker you'll be in the tub."

When he stood, every muscle in his body groaned in protest. His headache had worsened too, and it showed no sign of abating. But he knew she felt no better than he did. At least she seemed to be clear of whatever drug Santos had given her, but she was obviously close to exhaustion. "You're doing fine, you know. We've made good time."

"I can't tell," she answered. "Sometimes it seems like we've been walking for days. The worst part is that it all looks the same, so that you can't tell when you've left one place and come to another."

He hugged her. "Just in case you don't know, I'm proud of you, Anna. There are a lot of things I want to say . . ."

"I know," she whispered.

He adjusted their backpacks and they started walking again, setting their sights on the small goals—the next rise, the stretch where they could see agave growing in abundance, the tall silhouette of a boogum tree. At times it would have been easy to imagine that they wandered through an alien landscape, where every unnatural shape and texture posed a threat. He wished he felt more capable of dealing with whatever lay ahead.

Anna didn't seem to be bothered by the unfamiliar environment. Each time he looked at her, she had an encouraging smile to offer, and she instinctively kept their conversation turned away from any doubts she might have. "How old are you?" she asked him once.

"Thirty-eight. Why?"

"It just seems odd that I know so much of who you are, but none of the usual things."

"I told you once that where we're concerned, nothing is ordinary, remember?"

The rest of the day passed like that, one or the other of them asking questions, holding the answers close like a security blanket, searching for normality.

"Did you date a lot when you were in school?"

She shrugged. "Just my share, I guess. I wasn't a wall-flower, but I had more fun in groups, you know, going bowling or to the beach."

"I've never bowled and I always burn before I tan. Think we can work around it?"

"Maybe. It depends on whether you have any redeeming social value."

"You never mention your family. I don't even know if you have one."

"One brother, nine years older. He left home when I was a kid. And a father, if he's still alive. I haven't seen him since I enlisted."

"When was that?"

"A long, long time ago. I was seventeen, itching to see the world. A pig farm in Indiana just didn't fit in with what I wanted."

"Haven't you ever wanted to go home?"

"Not until now, with you."

"Tell me about Wynette. Is she all right?"

He laughed. "She'll always be all right. I've never seen anybody with so much energy. Or so much loyalty. We had to threaten her with knockout drops to keep her on the island."

"That's what you think. She'd have fought you to a standstill if she really thought her being here would help. You got off easy."

"Don't say that to Felix. He thinks he was asserting his male authority."

"Your grandfather arranged the engagement between you and Herrera, didn't he?"

"In a way. We both knew it was what he wanted, and there didn't seem to be any reason to disagree. Wynette asked me about it not long ago, wanted to know why I never seemed excited about getting married." Anna smiled at the memory. "She told me if a man was worth marrying, he should be worth getting excited about."

"Smart girl. Are you getting excited now?"

She stopped walking long enough to kiss him.

"Have you ever loved anyone?"

"You mean have I ever loved another woman besides you?"

"Yes."

"Once, in Southeast Asia. I was going to marry her."

"What happened?"

"She died, along with our son. He was eight months old."

"Will you tell me about her sometime?"

"Sure. I've already told her about you."

It was an odd remark, but she understood exactly what he meant.

"How do you feel about Herrera now?"

She looked at him askance. "The same as always. He's family and I love him."

"I think that's what I wanted to hear," he grinned.

"You don't have to hear anything, Donovan. You already know, so stop fishing."

That night they slept on the ground with no shelter except their love and a solar blanket.

"Come on, duchess. Drink your coffee. Only one cup to a customer."

She blinked her eyes, sat up sleepily and yawned. "I don't believe it. Room service yet." Taking the small tin cup from his hand, she sipped at the hot liquid cautiously. "Instant. My favorite flavor."

To her surprise, he'd even used some of the precious water to fix a pouch of powdered eggs. They were mostly tasteless, except for a hint of synthetic seasoning, but the food warmed her stomach and provided the energy she needed to face the brisk dawn air.

After breakfast they worked together to repack their survival kits and break camp. Then she worked some of the tangles out of her hair and rebraided it while he watched her.

"How do you do that without a mirror?"

"Practice, years and years of it. And native talent, of course."

The morning passed quickly. Though their bed had been hard and uncomfortable, the uninterrupted sleep had buoyed them up both physically and mentally. The foothills that were their ultimate destination seemed much nearer now, infinitely more attainable, and they marched steadily.

By midmorning the ground had become more uneven, once again sloping upward; ahead they could see the outline of the first small outcropping, and behind it the hills.

"How far do you think it is?" she asked.

"About a mile, maybe less." He stopped to tug at the straps running across his shoulders.

She waited for him, impatient to hurry on and see the end of their journey, as much for his sake as for hers. He didn't look well to her, and she knew the strain and exertion had taken a dreadful toll. Felix had told her the doctors in Salinas had recommended at least three days in the hospital, but Jay had threatened to walk out if they didn't discharge him. When they got home, she promised herself, she would force him to rest if it meant staying in bed with him twenty-four hours a day.

Soon the rocks were close enough that she could see a deep, hollowed-out spot that was deliciously shaded and cool looking. And the best thing was its size. She and Jay could rest there, maybe sleep for an hour before she had to put her mangled feet back on the ground.

"Look, Jay, isn't that the most beautiful sight you've ever seen? We can actually get out of the sun for a while."

Surprised when he didn't answer, she turned.

He had stopped, his stance one of taut alertness. His head was tilted, the familiar guarded look that she hated spread across his features. After a second, she knew why. The unmistakable sound of an engine raised the fine hairs on her neck.

To the northeast, the direction from which they had come, she could see a low cloud of dust. A vehicle, moving fast, bounced and bucked across the uneven terrain. In another moment she had identified it as a jeep; its three occupants jerked around like puppets each time the tires hit an obstacle.

"Could it be Tanner?" she asked, feeling Donovan's tension pulling at her.

"Maybe, but I'm not taking any chances." Dropping his backpack, he pulled the automatic from his belt.

She didn't wait for him to tell her to run. Her feet took flight, bringing the rest of her body along with no conscious action on her part. Jay's boots thudded behind her, punctuating her fear.

The ground seemed to have suddenly sprouted a million

new pitfalls, each of them designed to trip and snare her. She managed to jump over one small agave plant that had appeared out of nowhere, but when she hit the ground her ankle gave way and she stumbled. Donovan's hand shot out to steady her, but it was too late to halt her momentum.

She twisted, trying to avoid the larger agave, but its spines ripped through the tender flesh of her forearm. Frantic now, she fought to free herself from the vicious spikes.

Donovan grasped the waistband of her jeans and pulled, lifting her from the plant. Then they were racing once more for the relative safety of the outcropping. He pushed her through a narrow opening between two huge hunks of granite, over the lower rocks, until at last they were ringed by a natural fortress.

Anna collapsed against a boulder half again as tall as she, pressing her back against the warm stone while she brought her ragged breathing under control.

Donovan grasped her hands, turned them palms-up. They were marked with slashes, angry and red; beneath the new wounds, her skin was torn and scraped from the climb up the mountain the day before.

"We need to wash these cuts," Donovan told her. "Where's the canteen?"

"I thought you had it."

"Damn! I dropped it with the backpack. There was an extra in your gear."

"We emptied it this morning, remember?" She tried to touch his face, but her lacerated fingers shied away from the contact. "Jay, did you see who it is?"

"No. But I'll climb up there, take a look." He indicated the highest point in sight, relatively flat on top.

He swayed suddenly, capped his hands to his head.

"What's wrong?" she cried. "Jay, sit down, please. If you fall, I can't hold you . . ."

"I'm all right." Just speaking was an effort; his voice reverberated inside his head, distorted and deafening.

Then the sensation began to diminish as quickly as it had come. "The doctor said I might have headaches for a few days. Don't worry, it's over now."

She knew he was minimizing the situation, but what good would it do to argue. There was absolutely nothing either of them could do about it except try to survive.

"Why don't you rest for a minute," she suggested. "I'll go up and look."

"How can you climb with those hands?" he asked sharply.

"How can you climb with that head?" she retaliated.

A voice, loud and unwelcome, ended the debate.

"Donovan, we can end this now. There is no need to create further distress for the woman." Santos's words echoed off the granite walls, coming from all directions.

"Your concern is touching. I'm armed, Santos, and I won't mind killing you, not at all."

"You are foolish not to surrender now. We are three to two, and you are wounded. There is no way for you to get out."

"And you can't get in. Looks like a stalemate to me." Donovan checked the clip in his weapon, began inching his way along the granite, searching for a foothold.

"Not quite," Santos said. His voice seemed to be louder now. "We found the helicopter, Donovan. It seemed to be stocked with food and water. We also found your pack, with a full canteen inside. I am willing to wager that you have no water with you. If necessary, we can wait you out, Donovan."

"Jay," Anna whispered, "he didn't mention Felix or 'Tavio."

He nodded. "I heard. If he got them, he'd be bragging about it. Either they got away from the chopper before Santos found it, or Tanner's already picked them up."

"What is your decision, Donovan?" Santos shouted confidently. "Quickly or slowly, it makes no difference to me."

"I'm getting tired of this conversation, Santos." Donovan

finally found what he needed, a niche in the rock about three feet up. He placed the toe of his boot into the crack, boosted himself up. "I'd rather play a game. It's called shoot the pig in the head. Do you like games?"

"As you wish, Donovan. You are a clown, and clowns are invariably stupid."

Anna watched Donovan's slow ascent, holding her breath. Then a noise, like a sole scuffed against rock, spun her around. A figure was silhouetted against the pale blue sky, arm raised and pointing.

"Look out!" she screamed.

Donovan dropped beside her, fired the automatic almost in the same movement. The bullet found its mark and the impact sent the man reeling back, clutching his shoulder.

With a hoarse shout he disappeared from view. Anna heard him fall, then the noise subsided into a murmur of curses and finally faded away.

"He's not dead," she said, amazed at her disappointment. "What if he comes back?"

"He can't manage these rocks with only one arm. Besides, he's unarmed now." Donovan edged past her, cautiously climbed through the crevice and up into the rocks. In a moment he returned, holding the fallen gun.

He handed it to Anna. "Can you use it?"

She knew he wasn't referring to her mechanical knowledge. "If I have to," she answered, accepting the weapon. She stuck it into her waistband as she'd seen him do. "I'm not afraid of it."

"Come on, then." He took her arm, pulled her over to the base of the flattop. Kneeling, he motioned her to step on his shoulders, then he raised her carefully. "Stretch out your arms and lie against it," he ordered. "I'll push you as far as I can, then you should be able to crawl on over."

The granite was hot and rough, but Anna was more aware of Donovan's growing weakness. She felt his shoulders tremble under her feet, and when he grasped her shoes and began to push her up, she forced her fingertips into the small cracks, pulling her weight to relieve him of the burden.

As soon as she was secure, she turned to help him. He ignored her outstretched hands and made the climb alone. When he at last lay beside her, he was pale and exhausted.

He rested for too short a time, then he belly-crawled to the eastern rim, motioning her to follow.

Their vantage point was good. The rock jutted out almost like a ledge, higher than anything else in front of them. They could see the jeep parked a hundred yards away; a man sat slumped in the backseat.

Nearby stood Santos, in deep conversation with a third man. It was Crewe. He looked uncomfortable in the heat, wiping the sweat from his face and neck over and over again. Santos gestured toward the rocks and Crewe nodded.

Donovan watched as they separated. Santos headed around the outcropping, obviously looking for a new point of entry into the rocks. Crewe found the gap where Donovan and Anna had entered, squeezed his bulk through the crevice and disappeared.

Rolling onto his back, Donovan held his hand over his eyes. His head had become a block of agony, the glare of the sun nearly blinding him. "Listen to me. I'm going back down. If I can take Crewe first, we shouldn't have any problem getting Santos. He's too green to be effective on his own. I want you to stay here."

"No, I want to go with you."

"Damn it, Anna, that just gives me one more thing to worry about!" He regretted the words as soon as they were said. "I'm sorry, honey. But I need to know you're as safe as you can be. You can see everything from up here, and there's no way Santos can get to you without you seeing him first." He reached for her, held her close.

"All right," she said shakily. The thought of him being out of her sight for even a moment was almost more than she could bear, but she told herself that was selfishness. Let him do what he had to without more pressure from her.

"Good. If I can, I'll draw Santos around to the east side. Watch for him. If you can get a clear shot, take it." He caressed her cheek with his thumbs. "If something happens, go straight back, over the rocks. We're on a long slope up here; it should take you quite a way. Look for small, dark openings, where you could wedge yourself in out of sight. Santos can't check them all out. You could stay holed up for days."

She didn't point out the obvious—that without water there wouldn't be any use in hiding. She knew he'd already thought of it. Just one more thing they didn't talk about, because there was no way to change it.

He kissed her once, fiercely, then he slid away and dropped out of sight.

On her belly, she crawled back to the edge of the overhang. She could see neither Crewe nor Santos, and there was no sound to break the silence of the still heat. The man in the jeep had changed positions, was now examining his shoulder.

For a while Anna watched him, trying to keep her imagination at bay. It was all too easy to picture Donovan lying still and lifeless upon the equally lifeless rocks. She forced herself to keep her attention on the ground below, alert for any movement.

The man in the jeep suddenly raised his head. She thought at first he had spotted her, and her heart skipped. Then she realized his vision was trained in another direction, to her left. Turning her head, she peered at the mounds of granite, into their shadows, then she saw him.

Donovan's head and shoulders moved stealthily above one of the higher rocks, bobbing in and out of sight. From his stance, she could tell he was stalking Crewe. Her tongue became glued to the roof of her mouth, and she trembled violently.

The shrill blast of the jeep's horn cut through the brittle air, jerking her attention back to the wounded man. He was warning the others! Immediately shots rang out. She heard Crewe's roar of pain and rage, then he was quiet.

Pushing herself to her feet, she turned to run but stopped when she heard running footsteps below her. She fell prone, looked over the edge. It was Santos.

Getting to her knees, she pulled the gun from her waistband. He would be in the clear any second, and she might not get another chance. But the gun wobbled crazily. She couldn't grip it, and her hands shook so hard she almost dropped it.

Santos would be directly beneath her in a few more steps, three, two . . .

Without stopping to think, she jumped off the ledge. Her feet struck Santos's shoulders, pounding him into the hard earth, while she bounced and rolled a few feet away.

She was winded, but she managed to gain her feet. Santos was already standing, his eyes darting over the ground. He'd dropped his gun. Anna spotted it at the same time he did, and they both lunged for the weapon. Anna felt it in her fingers for just a moment, then a blow in her face knocked her away.

She found herself pinned upright against the rock wall, looking at Santos's face only inches from hers.

"At last," he said almost lovingly. "You have no idea how much pleasure this gives me." His fingers closed around her throat, forcing her chin up painfully.

"But why?" she whispered. "You must know by now that 'Tavio has contacted the government. They don't need my testimony anymore . . ."

"Yes, I know. It has been difficult to stay ahead of them, but I have managed. This has become a matter of personal satisfaction." He spoke conversationally, a faint smile on his lips. "You have cost me everything, Anna. Now you will pay for that loss."

His fingers tightened. With his other hand, he raised his gun, placed it to her temple.

The choke hold loosened abruptly. Anna looked past him. Donovan stood there, the barrel of his automatic pressed to the base of Santos's skull.

"Drop it. Now."

Santos complied, letting his gun fall from limp fingers.

Donovan's eyes at first appeared to be cold, but when Anna looked into them she could see a fire burning.

He pulled Santos around, placed the automatic against his temple. "Do you know what a nine-millimeter will do to your head, Santos?" His voice was unrecognizable. "Can you imagine how little will be left of your brain?"

Anna felt sick and cold. She couldn't bear what was happening. If she could stop it, she would. She had to, for Donovan's sake.

"No, Jay," she said quietly, moving to his side. "There's been too much violence, and we've been swept along because we had no choice." She swallowed, praying that her words would get through to him. "We have a choice now, darling. We won. It's over, and we won."

For one long, eternal moment she feared that he would pull the trigger. Then he blinked, looked at her. Finally, he relaxed.

"You're one lucky son of a bitch, Santos."

Anna wiggled her toes in the sand, loving the texture and coolness. It had been a long day and she needed this time to refresh herself, away from the guests, away from the chatter.

Gazing out at the lazy waves shimmering in the moonlight, she smiled to herself. Wynette had nearly had a fit when Anna told her she was going for a walk.

"A walk?" she said in astonishment. "Girl, this is your weddin' supper; you can't leave now."

"Sure I can," Anna had said cheerfully. "Don't worry, I won't be gone long, and nobody will miss me. Jay's not even here right now. Felix and 'Tavio drug him off somewhere for one last drink."

"Well, okay, but I think you're just plain crazy. I'd be soakin' up all this attention like a sponge."

Now she'd been out here far longer than she'd planned,

but she needed the solitude. The champagne had gone to her head, she guessed, but she thought this must be the most beautiful night in creation. Stars danced in the sky like diamonds, and the breeze flowed around her, heavy with a thousand delicious smells. She didn't want to relinquish the beauty, not yet. If only Jay were here to share it with her . . .

She felt another presence on the beach. Without looking, she knew who it was. Would it always be this way? she wondered; would she always be so aware of him that she would instinctively know where he was and what he was thinking? It was a comforting thought, that mystical link; she would never be alone again.

She turned slowly, her nerves tingling. He stood at the edge of the trees, his arms open and beckoning.

Run, Anna, run. And she did, right into his arms.

THE BEST IN SUSPENSE

BESTSELLING BOOKS FROM TOR